THE TAYLORS VERSION
Love Stories

Also by Elizabeth Eulberg

Young Adult

The Lonely Hearts Club

Prom and Prejudice

Take a Bow

Revenge of the Girl with the Great Personality

Better Off Friends

Just Another Girl

Past Perfect Life

Take a Chance On Me

Middle Grade

The Best Worst Summer

The Scared Silly Series

Curses Are the Worst

Zombie Wedding Crashers

Vampires Ruin Everything

The Great Shelby Holmes Series

The Great Shelby Holmes

The Great Shelby Holmes Meets Her Match

The Great Shelby Holmes and the Coldest Case

The Great Shelby Holmes and the Haunted Hound

THE TAYLORS VERSION
Love Stories

ELIZABETH EULBERG

SCHOLASTIC INC.

ISBN 978-1-5461-7673-2

10 9 8 7 6 5 4 3 2 1 25 26 27 28 29

Printed in the U.S.A. 40

First printing 2025

Book design by Stephanie Yang

For Jen Calonita—my Swiftie sister.
I can't imagine doing these books with anybody else. Who knew when we met all those years ago that our paths would align for the most perfect project?

You are forever and always made of starlight.

THE TAYLORS

Teffy

Taylor

Tay

TS

Our Chat (The Taylors Version)

TAYLOR🎊: Taylors! Are we ready to enter our High School Era?

TAY TAY🎉: YESSSSS! Meet here to discuss everything for OUR FIRST DAY OF HIGH SCHOOL

TS⚽: Gotta train

TAYLOR🎊: TS! You've got all day to train

TAY TAY🎉: You've been training ALLLLLLLL SUMMMMMMER!!!!!!

TAYLOR🎊: Just run to Tay Tay's!!!!

TEFFY📚: Please, TS. Say yes instead of no.

TAY TAY🎉: EXACTLY

TAYLOR🎊: Are you going to say no to our Teffy? AND ignore Mother's advice? REALLY?

TS⚽: Jeez . . . you know how to pressure a girl

TAYLOR🎊: Is that a yes?

TS⚽: Yes yes yes yes

TAY TAY🎉: That's the spirit!

ONE
the 1

"Welcome to high school, it's been waiting for us!" Tay Tay sings as she opens the front door to Teffy.

Teffy wishes she could be as excited as Tay Tay for high school, or anything, really. But this is why they get along so well. Tay Tay craves the spotlight and attention, while Teffy is happy sitting by herself reading and writing.

"Come here!" Tay Tay hugs Teffy tightly. "I know we practiced some older songs the other day, but when do I get my *next* Teffy masterpiece?"

"Soon, I hope," Teffy replies, even though she's been struggling. It's hard writing love songs when Teffy has never had a boyfriend. Just unrequited crushes. That's the best part about being a writer, she guesses. She gets to sit back and observe for inspiration. Although she feels that's all she's been doing lately.

Tay Tay leads Teffy down the hallway of her house, which Teffy knows about as well as her own. Tay Tay's has become the official gathering place for the Taylors since they met the first day of middle school. It's only her and her dad, so it's not swarming with siblings like Taylor's house. And it's next to an actual Christmas tree farm, so she's got a huge backyard as well as a pool.

"Oh, it smells really good," Teffy remarks as she takes a whiff of the warm spice-scented house. Tay Tay and her dad have gotten into baking during the past year, and the Taylors have been reaping the rewards—aka delicious cookies and brownies.

"We made chai cookies, Taylor's version, of course!" Tay Tay claps excitedly and does a little cheer. She's in full cheerleading mode: wearing a short pink pleated skirt, her tight brown curls up in two pom-poms. "But that's not all, look what I got you at Vintage."

Tay Tay runs over to the big couch in the center of the den and holds up a dark purple long-sleeved peasant top. "It's so *folklore*, right? It's so you!"

It is so Teffy. While Tay Tay's currently in her pastel *Lover* era, Teffy prefers the comfy, fall vibes of *folklore* and *evermore*. "It's perfect, thank you!"

Tay Tay sits in the middle of the floor, her brown legs crossed. "I figure you can pair it with some denim shorts and those cute black ankle boots."

Teffy plops down next to her. "Can you come up with all my outfits for the year?"

"You know you can't take that back now!" Tay Tay laughs as she bumps Teffy, then stops and studies her. "Is everything okay?"

"Yeah," Teffy replies, although probably not at all convincingly. "Just a bit nervous for tomorrow." Which is probably the biggest understatement of the year. Teffy is *terrified* of high school. Sure, she should be open to new possibilities, but she doesn't like change.

"Hey, remember what happened when you started middle school. You met me!"

"And me!" Taylor Perez comes storming into the den, her raven-colored hair bouncing in her wake. "The door was open— Oh! What is that delicious smell?" Taylor walks by Tay Tay and Teffy to go directly into the kitchen. "I'm assuming these cookies are for us?" She doesn't even bother waiting for an answer. "Well, they are now!" Taylor comes back with one cookie in her mouth and the others on a plate. "Where's TS?"

"She'll be here," Teffy replies, knowing TS will keep her word. She hopes.

Taylor hands Teffy and Tay Tay each their own cookie. "TS better be here." She says it like the threat it is. "I get that she's busy getting ready for soccer season, but we all have our own stuff."

Doesn't Teffy know it. Her friends are amazing. TS is a star athlete, so she's been busy all summer with a soccer league. Then there's Tay Tay, who has upped her gymnastics lessons to get ready to audition for the Harrison High School cheer squad, which Teffy knows she'll get. And Taylor is busy being Taylor. She spent this summer working for the parks and rec summer program. Teffy smiles thinking about how much Taylor loves bossing people around. And, well, she's really good at it. While Teffy . . . has her books and music. It's a quiet life. A drama-free life. She likes it. It's just that she sometimes feels like her friends have so much going on and Teffy will get left behind.

"Anyways." Taylor pulls a bracelet kit out of her backpack. "Let's get started. What bracelets are we going to make that say we're amazing, because of course we are, but freshmen and, like, super grown-up and stuff? How about 'Freshman Year' and, in parentheses, 'The Taylors Version'?"

"That's a little too long, even for us," Teffy says with a laugh.

"Okay, how about we do the initials so only *we* know what it means," Tay Tay replies.

"Yes!" Taylor dumps out the beads and starts getting to work. "Oh, and since we're all in the same first period, I'll get the whole Taylor thing out of the way, okay?"

The "Taylor thing" is what brought them together on the first day of middle school. It turns out having four Taylors—all named after Taylor Swift!—in one class made things confusing. So they used nicknames: Taylor Bennett picked Teffy, Taylor Johnson chose Tay Tay, and Taylor Perez insisted she get to keep her name. As the youngest of five kids, she's had to share everything and most of her clothes are hand-me-downs, so she wanted her name for herself. As for TS, her last name is Shaw, so it just sort of happened.

"Speaking of nicknames," Tay Tay starts as she stands up, "I feel like Tay Tay is *so* middle school, and now I want to be known simply as Tay. What do you think? Am I a Tay?" She then does a high kick.

"So *Tay*." Taylor nods along approvingly. "So very, very *high school*."

"Yeah, Tay," Teffy seconds, even though she knows it'll take her a while to get used to it.

There's a knock on the door. "Finally!" Taylor calls out.

Tay Tay, wait, *Tay* jumps up and opens the front door to find a sweat-stained TS in shorts and a T-shirt. Her face is nearly the same color as her bright red hair, which is pulled up tightly in a ponytail.

"Hey, Tay Tay," TS says before taking a swig from a water bottle.

"Oh, have you not heard?" Tay says with a wide smile. "I'm going by Tay now since I'm, like, so mature and stuff."

"Oh. Cool. But can *I* still be immature?" TS pulls her lips in to make a fishy face.

Tay throws her arm around TS. "We wouldn't want you any other way!"

"Phew." TS walks into the living room and starts stretching. "Hey."

"Did you *seriously* run here, TS? I was joking!" Taylor says with a roll of her brown eyes.

"I need to be in the best shape possible if I'm going to make the varsity squad . . . *and* start." Then TS takes out a disgusting green juice from her backpack.

"Ew! How can you drink that?" Tay's face scrunches up in disgust.

"You mean my *jug of excellence*? Look, you gotta take big swings to skip junior varsity as a freshman. And big sips!" She then takes another swig of the juice, and a trail of green makes its way down her cheek. "What can I say? I'm on a new regimen and I'm feeling great."

"And you're so going to make the team." Tay takes a big bite of her cookie.

"Thanks." TS sits down with her legs out straight and reaches for her toes. "And we all know you're going to make the cheer squad, Tay."

"I hope so, even though you all are abandoning me." Tay puts her hand dramatically to her forehead.

Teffy feels a pang of guilt, but as much as she liked cheering with the Taylors in middle school, she prefers the safety of the bleachers. Plus, it's not a Taylors thing anymore. TS dropped out in sixth grade to focus on soccer and Taylor announced this summer she wasn't going to try out by simply saying, "Pass."

Just another thing they won't have together in high school.

"But what if I don't make it?" Tay's face folds into a frown.

Taylor snorts. "Please. There are a few things we can all count on. One, Taylor Swift making an iconic album. Second, this one having her notebook on her to write lyrics." She gestures her chin at Teffy. "And three, you and TS making your teams."

"Go, Taylors!" Tay jumps up to do a split in midair.

"Exactly!" Taylor lets out a laugh. "I mean, *come on*."

Tay looks thoughtful for a moment. "I love that we have goals. Oh! Okay, let's all say what we want for freshman year. Oh, wait, even better. Let's make a *wish* and set our intentions for the new school year." Tay runs over to the counter where her dad keeps his keys and spare change. She digs for a few seconds, before holding up four pennies triumphantly. "Let's go!"

When the door to the backyard opens, Teffy is hit with the warmth of the August air and the familiar smell of chlorine from the pool. Teffy smiles at all the memories they've had in this backyard, lounging on the wicker furniture—Teffy and TS usually seeking shelter from the sun under one of the big umbrellas. They've done so much here, from barbecues to singing along to their favorite Taylor Swift songs, which is, like, all of them. Teffy holds the memories close to her, hoping that things won't change too much now that they're in high school.

Taylor throws her arm around Teffy, giving her a squeeze. Like she could read her mind. TS gives her a hip bump, while Tay steps forward, holding her penny close to her chest.

"I'll start." Tay closes her eyes, then gives herself a nod before opening them. "This year, I will make the cheer squad . . . obviously, but also I want to start a band with Teffy."

Teffy's stomach drops out, remembering the disaster that was the seventh-grade talent show. "How about I just keep writing the songs?"

"But you're such an amazing piano and guitar player. *Please.*" Tay bats her eyelashes. It's what she does to get her father to cave. Teffy, however, won't give in that easily. Tay drops her penny into the pool. "Well, I guess it's up to the universe now."

"I'm next," Taylor declares. "I'm going to rule the school."

"And that's different from middle school, how?" TS asks with a laugh.

Taylor turns toward her friends. "Taylors, I hereby officially declare that I am running for freshman class president." She tosses her penny in.

"Oh my goodness, that's so perfect." Tay does a cheer.

It is perfect, Teffy thinks. Taylor would make the best

representative for their class. Yes, she's opinionated, but she'll also stick up for someone in need. She's often Teffy's voice when she has trouble speaking up for herself.

"As for me," TS begins. She looks down at the rippling water. "I am going to help the varsity girls' soccer team win state." She then throws her penny high up in the air and, with the grace that has come from years of practicing, kicks it squarely into the center of the pool.

"Goooooooal!" Tay cheers.

"What about you, Teffy?" TS asks.

Teffy looks at the penny in her hand. Her heart starts beating faster. The thing is, Teffy does have something she really wants this year, but she's too scared to say it aloud, even to the Taylors. She wishes she could be as confident as her friends, but this isn't something she can get by hard work. She scrambles to come up with something to say. "Um, maybe get a job at By the Book?"

"Boring!" Taylor says with a tsk. "This is *high school*. It needs to be something *fun*."

"Like starting a band with me!" Tay sings.

Teffy can feel her cheeks getting red. She closes her eyes and she holds the penny up to her heart. She takes a deep breath, makes a wish, and tosses the penny into the pool.

"Well, what did you wish for?" Taylor asks impatiently.

TS playfully smacks Taylor on the shoulder. "Stop being so nosy. Teffy will tell us whenever she wants."

Teffy gives TS a grateful smile.

"Fair enough. Okay, Taylors, let's bring it in." Taylor holds her hand out and the three others pile their hands on top of one another's. "Here's to an amazing start to high school."

"One, two, three, let's go, Taylors!"

When Teffy arrives home, she's struck by how much quieter the Bennett house is than Tay's. Her older brother, Charlie, must still be out, and her parents have been spending more and more time at their store, Harrison by Design.

Teffy heads up to her bedroom. Before she turns on her lights, she sees Liam Yoon in his bedroom, which faces hers. The Yoon and the Bennett families are practically inseparable. The parents are best friends. Alex Yoon is one of Charlie's closest friends. Jae, the youngest Yoon, is a fellow Swiftie, so she and Teffy always have lots to talk about. And Teffy and Liam . . . well, he's her best non-Taylor friend. The two families go on summer holidays together and have Sunday dinners.

Teffy pauses for a moment to study Liam, even though she knows every detail of his face: the slope of his nose, his sharp, defined jaw, his dark eyes, and his full lips. She flickers her lights on and off to get Liam's attention. He looks up from his computer and smiles warmly at Teffy. He gives her a little wave, and just like that, her heart is practically pounding out of her chest.

Liam holds up a finger while he starts rummaging through his clothes. Liam has one of the messiest rooms Teffy has ever seen, and she's Charlie Bennett's sister! Teffy grabs her phone, waiting for a text. Instead, Liam triumphantly holds up a whiteboard. Teffy starts laughing. She and Liam used to write each other notes back and forth when they were younger.

Look what I found! Liam writes.

Teffy grabs her whiteboard, excited at the possibility of starting this tradition again. She wants to hold on tightly to her time with him. They used to ride the school bus together, but that stopped last year since Liam's a year older. Then Liam became busy with football and basketball and his friends and Cat. His girlfriend. Teffy swallows like there's a bad taste in her mouth.

Liam holds up the board. *Excited for HS?*

Teffy grimaces, which makes Liam laugh. Even from this distance, she can see his eyes sparkle. Liam runs his hands through his messy black hair before he writes again.

You got this

Teffy wishes she was as confident as everybody else about high school. It was Liam who had helped her on the first day of middle school. Teffy writes back, *I'm going to need another pep talk.*

Liam replies, *Anything for you, Tefs*

Teffy's stomach drops out. She thinks about that wish she made in the pool. The one she wouldn't share.

What Teffy wants more than anything is for Liam Yoon to realize that she's utterly in love with him and for him to love her back.

Our Chat (The Taylors Version)

TAYLOR🐝: Today is the day! Meet at my locker

TAY🎉: IT'S FINALLY HAPPENING!!!

TS⚽: Oh yay school

TAY🎉: TS! This is a BIG DEAL

TS⚽: Love you Tay, but you think everything is a BIG DEAL

TAY🎉: This IS

TEFFY📚: 😨

TS⚽: Take a deep breath, Teffy

TAYLOR🐝: We got your back

TAYLOR🐝: Now let's get ready to own high school

TWO
Fifteen

You've got this. You're strong. You're confident. You're Taylor Perez.

Taylor repeats this mantra to calm down any nerves she has about starting high school. Sure, she's a bit anxious, but nothing compared to her friends. As they gather at her locker, Taylor is sure to give each of them a hug. Tay's buzzing with nervous energy. Teffy looks like a scared kitten—her brown eyes darting around the loud, crowded hallway. TS chews on gum like she's trying to win a medal, which, knowing TS, she just might be.

"Anybody else overwhelmed?" Teffy asks in a small voice, but the others all nod in agreement.

A surge of protectiveness rushes through Taylor. No matter what, Taylor is going to make sure her friends are looked after. As the youngest of five kids, Taylor always had her siblings to protect her, and sometimes baby her. Taylor is many things, but she is *not* a baby. It's because of those very loud siblings that Taylor feels she needs to be extra to stand out. She doesn't want to be known as someone's sibling or someone's child, she wants to be known for being Taylor Perez. Her own person. Yes, she's one of the Taylors, but she likes having this chosen family of friends. Friends who are all starting this new high school journey.

Friends who Taylor is going to protect.

That gives Taylor the boost of confidence she needs. She counts to ten, then takes a deep breath. "We've got this, Taylors. Let's go."

Taylor leads her friends through the crowded hallway of Harrison High School. She can't help but smile at the double takes she's getting. Taylor filled out a bit over the summer. As she got ready this morning, she didn't see a baby in the mirror, she saw a young woman. Taylor decided that her high school vibe is going to be fun, a little flirty. She's now feeling very *Red/1989*. She wants to be effortlessly stylish, which is hard when she's stuck with her siblings' hand-me-downs. She took an old, oversized white NYC T-shirt from her brother and cut it up so it hangs off one shoulder, then paired it with black rolled-up boyfriend jeans and, of course, a bright red lip. She trimmed her dark brown wavy hair this summer so it skims her collarbones, and got long bangs.

"I can't believe this is happening!" Tay says as they walk into their first class of the day, American history.

"Oh, it's happening." Taylor nods at the back row of four seats and takes them for the Taylors.

Teffy sits and immediately gets out her notebook for class, while TS sets down the most obnoxiously huge water bottle on her desk. Tay breaks out a pastel notebook, which matches her pink-and-blue dress. Taylor loves how predictable her friends are.

"Good morning, class." A woman comes into the room, glasses perched on her head like a headband. "I'm Miss Prince, and welcome to American history. I'm going to start with attendance so I can start putting faces to names."

"Miss Prince," Taylor starts as she raises her hand. Every single head in the classroom has turned around to look at her. Unlike Teffy, she doesn't mind the attention.

"Yes, um—" Miss Prince looks down at a piece of paper.

"Taylor Perez, ma'am, I just thought I'd save you some trouble." Taylor smiles widely, especially since most of the class has seen her do this on the first day each year. "As you'll notice, you have four Taylors in this class."

"Taylor Johnson!" Tay says with a wave and bright smile.

"Taylor Shaw." TS holds up her finger.

The room goes quiet as those in the know glance at Teffy, who looks like a deer caught in headlights. Poor Teffy. It's gone downhill since the seventh-grade talent show. She gets quieter with each year. Same thing happened to Taylor's sister in high school. She became more self-conscious. Why do girls have to become smaller to make others comfortable? It's not something Taylor Swift has ever done and it's certainly not going to happen with *this* Taylor.

Taylor swoops in to prevent Teffy from having to talk if she's not ready. "And that's Taylor Bennett. We have nicknames to help you tell us apart. I'm Taylor."

"Tay!" Tay shouts with her arms stretched out above her head. She really is going to make the best cheerleader.

TS raises her hand. "TS."

“And this is Teffy.” Taylor gestures at a silent Teffy next to her. “We’re the Taylors.” Then, because she can’t keep it in and wants to start campaigning *now,* she stands up. Plus, what better class to do this in than history, since Taylor plans on becoming a big part of it. “And I’d like to take this moment to announce that I’ll be running for class president. Vote for Taylor!”

What Taylor doesn’t share is that this is going to be the year the Taylors will be entering their best era.

High school doesn’t stand a chance.

Taylor is already loving high school. Her first three classes were a breeze, she had not one, but *two* different boys start talking to her—they are cute, but she’s known both Zach and Jacob since first grade.

Taylor never doubted high school would be anything but amazing. She’s walking to fourth period, an extra sway in her hips, when she realizes that the numbers on the rooms are going in a different direction. She glances at the clock on the wall, revealing Taylor has less than two minutes to get to class. She can’t be lost, can she? Taylor doesn’t get lost.

She smiles to herself, as she will not show panic on her face. She simply needs to do a U-turn in the hallway, which has gotten less crowded since most people already found their classes. Taylor quickly turns around and slams right into someone. Her books go scattering across the floor.

“Sorry!” she squeaks out. No, Taylor doesn’t squeak. She also doesn't blurt out apologies, that's a Teffy thing—she once apologized to a chair she bumped into.

Taylor bends down to pick up her books, and the person she bumped into stoops down to help. "I've got—" she begins, but then sees the most gorgeous boy kneeling right next to her. He has short, sandy-brown hair, these pale hazel eyes, a dimple on his chin, and a hint of stubble.

"Let me help you," he says, his voice deep.

"Thanks, I'm new here." Taylor curses herself for sounding helpless.

"Oh, I know." He gives her a smile and Taylor can't help but notice how full his lips are.

"How?" she asks as they both stand up, and she's not surprised to find he's a foot taller than her.

"Well, that's easy. I haven't seen you before, and I'd definitely remember."

Is this really happening? Tay and Teffy are the ones who love watching rom-coms and dreaming of meet-cutes, and here Taylor is bumping into a gorgeous older boy her first morning. Because no way is he in her grade.

"Where are you headed?" he asks as he takes Taylor's schedule from her. "Ah, freshman lit." Is Taylor imagining it or are his eyes actually sparkling? "That's down the hallway. Here, let me walk you."

"Won't you be late for class?" What is she even doing? *Just let him walk you!*

"Some things are worth a late slip." The guy starts strolling down the hallway and Taylor is so hypnotized that she follows him. "What's your name?"

"Taylor." This might be the first time in history that Taylor Perez is at a loss for words.

"Hey, Taylor, I'm Hunter, and as a senior, I volunteer to be your guide. Anything you need, come find me." He then stops in front of a door, which Taylor realizes is the room she needs.

"Thanks."

"Well, Taylor, I guess you owe me now." Hunter winks at her before turning back down the hallway. She actually yelps when the class bell buzzes seconds later.

Yeah, Taylor may have high school figured out. However, that intense feeling in her stomach? *That* is something new.

"Over here!" Taylor calls out to the other Taylors, who are scanning the crowded cafeteria. Taylor practically ran out of her last class to grab a table. She cannot wait to tell the Taylors about Hunter.

She can hardly contain herself as she waits for them to get settled. TS, who broke a middle-school record in track for both girls and boys, is walking at a glacial pace.

"How is it possible that I already have so much homework," Tay starts as she sits down. "And I still have three classes to go? I just want it to be cheer auditions already. I can only be nervous about so many things."

“Tay, you’ve totally got this,” Teffy says as she slides in next to Taylor.

TS finally arrives at the table. “Yeah, I’m pretty sure if you google ‘cheerleader,’ you come up. You’re basically a walking cheering section.”

“Aww.” Tay hugs TS. “How was your morning, TS?”

“I’m counting down hours until practice today.” TS places a green insulated lunch bag on the table.

“Same, especially since I’m dreading next period. Biology.” Tay sticks her tongue out in disgust.

“I had it this morning, if you need help—” Teffy begins, but Taylor can’t keep it in anymore.

“You’re not going to believe what happened to me!” she practically shouts. A few heads turn at the next table, but she doesn’t care. “I was walking . . .” she starts, but notices Hunter stride into the cafeteria. Taylor thought *she* walked with confidence, but Hunter is on a whole other level. She can’t help but be mesmerized by him. Hunter’s eyes scan the room and stop when he spots Taylor. She’s about to look away—she can’t believe she got caught *gawking*—but he’s walking over to her. *Her!*

“Oh my goodness, oh my goodness, he’s coming over,” Taylor says under her breath. Her heart is hammering so quickly in her chest, she’s worried it may explode.

“Who?” Tay asks as she turns around.

“Don’t look!” Taylor hisses.

TS’s brows furrow. “Um, you okay there, Taylor?”

Is she? Taylor has no idea. She's never been this uncertain and out of sorts before. She kind of likes it.

"Hey, Taylor." Hunter slides in next to her. "How's lunch?"

Taylor can hardly speak. Hunter's entire focus is on her, his eyes blazing into hers. She can tell the other Taylors are exchanging confused looks.

"Good." What is it about Hunter that makes her so quiet?

"And your class? That you made on time." He smiles, causing the corners of his eyes to crinkle.

"Good."

Hunter's lips curl as he looks around the table. "And who do we have here?"

"I'm TS and exactly how old are you?" TS is never one to beat around the bush.

Hunter lets out a laugh. "Seventeen. Nice to meet you, TS. Who else do we have . . ."

Taylor is mute as her friends introduce themselves. Even Teffy is talking, while Taylor's transfixed by Hunter, trying to memorize every detail of him. He smells like cologne. Most of the boys her age smell gross, like they haven't even heard of deodorant. Hunter's hair is styled but messy. He's wearing a distressed black T-shirt that shows off muscles—*he has muscles!* He casually slings his arm around Taylor and she has to keep reminding herself to breathe.

"Well, nice to meet you all." Hunter gives them a huge smile before turning back to her. "So, Taylor, can I see your phone?"

"My phone?" she asks, like she doesn't know what a phone is. She finally snaps out of it by digging her red-painted fingernails into her hands. "Yeah. Sure."

She hands him her phone and tries to seem cool . . . and hide her trembling hands.

Hunter types on her phone and then hands it back. "Now you have my number. And I sent myself a text so I have yours. Talk soon." He drums his fingers on the table for a second before getting up and heading to another table in the far corner.

"Okay, what's the deal with that guy?" TS asks, clearly not impressed.

"Yeah, he seems really nice, but, like, a bit too old," Teffy says in a quiet voice.

"Hunter's a *senior*," Taylor replies in awe.

"Ew." TS scrunches her nose. "That's a bit ick, Taylor."

"What? No, it's not! He's so cute! No, cute is for puppies, Hunter is *gorgeous*." Taylor can't believe her luck. Hunter has the pick of pretty much any girl in this school—how could he not with that smile and eyes and . . . just everything—and he chose to sit down and talk to *her*. Taylor notices a few curious looks at her from other tables.

While her friends spend the rest of lunch talking about their mornings and upcoming auditions, Taylor pushes her lunch away. She can only think about Hunter. She's never gone on a date. She's never even kissed a boy. And now . . . well, she doesn't want to get ahead of herself, but why else would Hunter ask for her number?

Taylor is practically gliding out of the cafeteria when a tall girl with long black hair stands in front of her. The girl's arms are crossed.

Taylor stands up straighter, her confidence back. "Yes? Can I help you?"

"You should watch out for Hunter. He's trouble, and I'm speaking from experience." The girl turns her back on Taylor and walks quickly down the hall.

Hunter? Trouble? What does that even mean?

There's part of Taylor that wants to run after the girl and demand she explain herself. But Taylor is a good judge of character, look at her friends! No, she can sense a kindness in Hunter. After all, he helped her when she was lost, even though it probably made him late to his class.

No, Hunter's not trouble.

That girl is just jealous.

Our Chat (The Taylors Version)

TAY🎉: I know we JUST said bye, but wish me luck 😳

TEFFY📚: I promise you, bio will be fine. We got put into pairs almost right away.

TAYLOR🐝: I'm with Tay, biology, meh but the LAW OF ATTRACTION

TS⚽: Get to class

THREE
Treacherous

This is it. Tay knows this is going to be the Best. Year. Ever. One, she's pretty sure she's going to make the cheer squad. She attended every rehearsal this past summer. Nailed all the routines. Practiced every day. Even this morning on her way to second period, Cat Sullivan, a sophomore cheerleader, stopped to say hello to her. Second, she is going to get Teffy to start a band with her. Okay, so their first—and only—performance during the seventh-grade recital didn't go well, but everybody makes mistakes! Tay dreams of being just like Taylor Swift—who doesn't? Tay has the voice and stage presence. She needs those amazing songs. And Teffy writes the best ones, they remind her of early Taylor. Acoustic guitar, singing of wanting someone.

Plus, Tay prefers doing things in a group. It's why she likes being on a cheerleading *squad*. Why she loves being with the Taylors. Why she wants Teffy to be by her side when she hits the stage and becomes a major superstar. Everything's better when you get to share it with the people you care about.

Tay's wants are so close to happening she can feel them within her grasp.

There's just one teeny, tiny obstacle in her way of making this the most perfect year: biology. Tay loves school, it's just that she finds science so boring. She missed out on the honor roll last year because of her C in science. Tay cringes when she thinks about her dad's reaction when he saw her report card. He didn't say he was disappointed, but she could tell by his face. Tay never wants to let her dad down. It's just been him and her since she could remember, so she's a total daddy's girl.

Tay walks to biology as if she's tiptoeing on the edge of a cliff. She's a bundle of dread and nerves when she enters the classroom. Then it's as if she's been given a lifeline when she spies familiar faces. Cat is sitting in the back with Tiffany and Becca, two other sophomore cheerleaders, who are wearing nearly identical outfits: denim skirts and tank tops, their hair in that cheerleader high pony.

"Hey, y'all!" Tay says brightly as she dares to sit right next to Cat. "You didn't take bio last year?"

"Hey, Tay!" Cat greets her warmly. "We did chemistry as freshmen."

Ugh, Tay dreads that more, if that's even possible.

"But more importantly, are you ready for practice?" Cat asks, her shiny blonde hair curled to perfection. While the Taylors tease Tay about being a walking definition of a cheerleader, Cat is the epitome. She always looks flawless—today she's wearing a crisp white sundress. White! In school. And she knows it'll stay that way.

"Yes, totally ready!" Tay says brightly, trying to conceal her nerves.

Cat leans in. "Well, you're a natural and it's so obvious you've put in the work. You've got my vote." Cat then lines up a notebook, pens, a water bottle, and hand sanitizer on her desk.

After that compliment, Tay finds herself sitting a little taller in her seat. She's always tried to have the posture of a dancer. Shoulders back, neck long.

"All right, class." The teacher in the front of the room ruins Tay's moment. He's older with a shock of white hair around the crown of his head. "I'm Mr. Wilson, welcome to biology."

Tay has decided she needs to be positive. She will not let biology ruin her mood. She breaks out her notebook and her color-coded system, and starts making notes, but as the teacher begins talking about cells, and DNA, and protein . . . Tay wishes she was in any other class.

Before she knows it, Mr. Wilson is already assigning their first project, which has something to do with prokaryotic cells, whatever those are. Tay glances at Cat, hoping Mr. Wilson will assign partners based on where they're sitting.

But as he looks toward a sheet, Tay realizes she is not going to be that lucky.

"Taylor Johnson?" Mr. Wilson calls out.

"Yes?" Tay replies, willing him to say Cat's name.

"I'm going to pair you with . . . Reece Matthews."

Tay looks around the room to find her new partner but sees mostly unfamiliar faces.

"It's emo boy over there," Becca says with an eye roll.

While the rest of the class get up and move toward their partners,

Tay's attention goes to a boy huddled over a notebook, wearing all black. His long black bangs cover his face. So biology *could* get worse.

"Poor Tay." Cat places her hand on top of Tay's. "Listen, you have any problems, you just ask us, okay? We cheerleaders stick together."

"Thanks!" Tay gives her a hopeful smile as she goes over to her new partner.

No, Tay will be positive! She's a people person and knew she'd be making new friends this year. She can win anybody over.

Tay pulls over a chair to him. "Hey, Reece, I'm Tay!"

Reece replies by continuing to write in his notebook, his hands ink-stained.

"Wow, I thought I took lots of notes," Tay remarks as she notices his notebook is filled with writing. Maybe she did get lucky and he's some genius who can help with her grade. She looks down at the sheet Mr. Wilson handed out. "Did you already figure all this out?"

Reece finally looks up from his notebook, and it's the first time Tay sees his face. She's nearly knocked over when he looks at her. Eye to eye, she can see he's got these crystal-clear blue eyes that stand out on his pale skin. Tay always thought TS was the palest person she's ever seen, but this guy is practically translucent.

"Nope, I'm working on lyrics." His attention returns to his notebook.

"Really? You write lyrics? So does my friend Teffy! She actually writes songs for me. I sing. You?" Tay realizes they should be focused on their assignment, but she also knows it's polite to get to know someone. Tay hasn't really met many people who are as into making music as she and Teffy.

"I'm in a band."

"You're in a band!" Tay says just a little too loudly, causing Mr. Wilson to look up from his desk. She clears her throat as she looks at the piece of paper.

"Yeah, the Archers."

THE ARCHERS! Is Reece for real? Tay nearly falls over. "The Archer" is one of her favorite songs from *Lover*, which is one of her favorite Taylor Swift albums. Although truthfully, they're all her favorite, but Tay would live in a pastel bubblegum world if she could.

"Oh my goodness!" Tay tries to keep her voice low. "What instrument do you play? Do you sing? What kind of music? Have you done gigs?" Tay knows she's being extra, but she's noticed Reece's shoulders have relaxed since she started bombarding him with questions.

"I sing and play guitar." He studies Tay for a moment and then continues, gesturing excitedly with his hands. "We pretty much play everything. Rock. Folk. Indie. I think it's the only way to become a better musician. Sometimes we play my original music."

"That's so cool." See, Tay knew high school was the perfect time to start a band. All she needs to do is convince Teffy. Which she knows will be a challenge. But Tay is up for it.

"What kind of music do you and your friend do?" Reece looks up at her from between his long bangs.

"Well, Teffy can pretty much do it all. She has her glittery gel pen moments but has really been into more of a fountain pen mood lately."

Reece's lips twitch. "I have no idea what any of that means."

Tay can't help but laugh. She's feeling much more optimistic about biology now.

"Well . . ." Reece fiddles with a black leather bracelet on his right wrist. "We're playing this weekend at a party. You should come."

Oh wow, *wow.* It's Tay's first day of school and she's already being invited to a party. To listen to a band! Before she shouts *YES!*, Tay thinks of her dad. He's very protective of her. She doubts he'd let her go to a party.

Then there's Reece. He's different from anybody Tay has met before. He's the opposite of her bright and colorful personality. She's the good girl who does what her father says. And, well, Reece seems like a bit of a bad boy. At least that's the vibe he's giving off: brooding, quiet, wearing all black . . .

"Here." Reece rips a piece of paper from his notebook and starts scribbling before handing it over to Tay. "Details."

She looks at the address and date, then she notices a phone number.

"Is this your number?" she asks. It probably would be good for her to have it if they're going to be biology partners.

"In case you want to hang."

Yeah, Tay's dad *definitely* won't like this.

Our Chat (The Taylors Version)

TAYLOR🐝: Good luck today, Tay and TS! You've both got this!

TEFFY📚: Can't wait to cheer you both on!

TAY🎉: Thanks! Um, WANT TO GO TO A PARTY THIS SAT?!?!?!

TAYLOR🐝: WHAT? And YES obvs!!! Maybe Hunter will be there? Can I invite him?

TS⚽: I'll be too busy starting on varsity

TAYLOR🐝: Yeah, you will. But also YOU ARE ALLOWED TO HAVE FUN

TS⚽: I'll celebrate when I'm on Team USA and we win the World Cup

TAYLOR🐝: Jeez, dream bigger, why don't you!

TAY🎉: This is why we love you, TS. DREAM BIGGEST!

TEFFY📚: Party? I don't think my parents will let me.

TAYLOR🐝: Just tell them we're spending the night at Tay Tay's

TAY🎉: It's TAY, remember? And OH! SLEEPOVER! YESSSS!!! Come on . . .

TAYLOR🐝: YES! Always yes! Come on Teffy

TEFFY📚: Maybe.

TAYLOR🐝: 😌

TAYLOR🐝: TS?

TS⚽: Gotta practice . . . 👏👏👏

TAYLOR🐝: She's a girl on a mission

FOUR
A Place in this World

TS silences her phone. She needs to concentrate; that means no distractions and definitely no parties. It's not like she doesn't want to spend time with the Taylors, it's just she needs to make the best impression with Coach Callahan to have a shot at making the varsity team.

She puts on her headphones and blasts her hype song, which she's played before every practice and match since forever: ". . . Ready for It?" Because of course it is.

TS *is* ready. She knows what she wants: to get on the varsity team as a freshman and start. To make a name for herself as one of the top athletes at Harrison High. In the state of Indiana. To go on and become one of those greats who only go by one name: Simone, Serena, Mia . . .

And greats, period. No "best female," simply the GOAT.

It's everywhere else in her life that TS isn't sure where she fits in. On the field, she belongs. Same with the Taylors. But beyond soccer and her friends . . .

Not like she needs anything else.

Besides, TS has a feeling she's made the team. She's the only freshman who hasn't been cut. Which didn't surprise her. Being an athlete is more than protein shakes and working out. It's studying, and she's been studying the Harrison Eagles girls' soccer team since she started kicking a ball. She's analyzed Coach Callahan's strategy. She's played with or against most of the other players on the team—she always played above her age level as that's how to get better. She's worked on her speed, since that's something the team lacked last year.

TS begins to stretch on the field. She feels the sun on her skin and rolls up the sleeves on her Team Taylors shirt they made last year. The sleeves have each of their nicknames written in a heart. TS's attention goes to the other side of the field, where the cheerleaders are practicing flips. Tay waves excitedly over to TS, who nods in return.

There's a part of TS that can't believe she was on the cheerleading squad in fifth grade. That she would do anything that took away from her soccer time, but her focus really shifted this last year. She's getting to an age when she can start being recognized by college coaches, even the national team. So no more goofing around—well, maybe *some*, but when TS is on the field, she's focused. Not that TS thinks being a cheerleader is easy. Tay is as much an athlete as TS.

Although it's not fair that the cheerleaders only cheer for the boys' teams. Because the thing is, the Harrison Eagles girls' soccer team is amazing. They've been to state the last three years. They're the ones who deserve the crowds and people cheering their names.

Alas, the patriarchy.

Coach Callahan blows her whistle and TS takes her headphones off and gets in a circle with the rest of the players.

"Okay! We're going to run some drills," Coach starts, to the groan of a few of the other girls. But TS can't wait to get out there and show what she's made of. What she's been practicing.

Whenever TS takes the field, she leaves it all on the table. Today will be no different.

She sprints so hard, her legs start burning, making her feel alive. She dribbles as if it's second nature to her. She runs so fast down the field, her ponytail whips around like she's flying. She suppresses a smile when she steals the ball away from a senior. When all the training comes together like this, TS feels invincible. She even does a few fancy taps with the ball. Okay, maybe she's showing off, just a little. However, she's proving that not only does she deserve to be there, but she should start.

"Let's go, Shaw!" Coach calls out as TS breaks away, yet again, and goes racing toward the goal, leaving the other players in her dust. She slows down a little bit, just to give them the (false) sense that they can catch up to her. She pulls back her leg to kick when there's a haze of lavender that takes the ball away.

There's a moment of shock when TS realizes the ball is no longer at her feet. She quickly snaps out of it and goes after this girl TS doesn't recognize. She's small but strong, with short, lavender hair pulled back in a headband. TS chases after her, trying to get the ball—and a small part of her pride—back. TS was so sure of herself, she let her guard down for a moment and she lost the ball.

Once TS gets closer to the player, it's like she's in some weird daze. There's quick feet from both the girls, it's almost like they're each anticipating what the other is going to do. TS is impressed and also relieved that this player will be on the same team.

The girl looks up for a moment, and TS uses that moment to get the ball back and sprint until she scores a goal.

Her fellow yellow-shirted teammates all cheer like she just won the big game, but TS is looking out on the field for the future teammate who almost bested her.

The girl catches up, her cheeks flush, a smile on her face that makes TS's belly toss. She holds her hand out to TS. "Not bad for an American," the girl says in a British accent. She gives TS a nod of respect. "I'm Gemma."

"Taylor, you can call me—"

"Shaw," Gemma says. "I heard Coach cheering you on."

"So you—" TS begins, but Coach cuts her off, bringing the team back in.

While TS should be listening to Coach, she can't help but steal glances at this new girl.

Hmm. Maybe some distractions are okay.

As she's more than proven, TS knows how to study: plays, opponents, and, yes, even her fellow teammates. Like her namesake, TS doesn't do anything by halves.

What TS has learned about Gemma Walker so far: She's a sophomore, her mom (who Gemma adorably refers to as *mum*) transferred from Oxford to Purdue University, as she's some famous engineering professor. They moved closer to Indianapolis since her father does pharmaceutical research for Eli Lilly. Gemma is just as impressive. She was selected to be part of the Chelsea FC Women's Academy, which is one of the top developmental programs in the UK. Her social media profile is a lot like TS's: filled with pictures of her teammates and friends. Her hair is dyed in different colors each season. TS is so jealous because she wanted to dye her hair like Megan Rapinoe, but her mom held up TS's naturally red hair and told her, "You never touch this gorgeous color." It does make getting ready for school easy, as she usually just throws it up in a ponytail.

"Try to keep up, Shaw," Gemma says to TS now during Friday's practice.

It's been like that all week. TS loves that someone is there to challenge her. It'll make her a better player.

And today is the day TS finds out if she's made the team.

TS keeps bouncing back and forth between being excited for the team roster to be announced and dread that she doesn't make it.

She *has* to make it.

As Gemma runs a drill, TS is mesmerized by how confident she is in her dribbling, how she bites the corner of her red lips when she's concentrating, how her green eyes—

"Shaw!" Coach yells. "You paying attention or is there something more important?"

Heat rises in TS's cheeks—with her pale coloring, it's difficult to hide when she gets embarrassed, which is why TS rarely allows for anything in her life that isn't sports or the Taylors. While Taylor spent all week talking about that senior guy Hunter—*boring*—TS has never let herself get carried away by relationships—especially romantic ones.

TS likes to focus on things she can control, like her speed and passing rate.

Coach blows the whistle signaling the end of practice. "Let's huddle!"

TS runs over, her stomach twisting in knots, hoping that one tiny slipup won't make Coach cut her.

"Great hustle out there." Coach gives them a nod. "Look around at the girls surrounding you, because they are all your teammates for the season."

Wait.

It takes TS a second to realize what that means. She did it. TS made *varsity*. As a *freshman*. She and Gemma are the only underclassmen who've done it.

TS jumps up in the air and pumps her fist. She's usually exhausted after practice, but her adrenaline is racing with the news.

Gemma gives TS a hip bump.

Scratch that. TS's entire body is about to explode from . . . just everything. The team. Gemma. It's all coming together. She feels like she could run a marathon.

Making varsity: DONE!

Next: starting!

After they've been dismissed, Gemma walks with TS to the sideline. "So, Shaw, what are you doing this weekend?"

"Training," TS replies automatically. It's pretty much her answer when anybody asks her what she's doing because that's what she's always working on: running, strength, passing. And it's clearly worked. But then again, Gemma isn't just anybody. TS wants to impress her with her dedication to the team.

"That's why you're so good." Gemma pulls her headband off and tosses her hair. The smell of lavender cuts through the scent of twenty girls running around for an hour. TS never paid attention to her own shampoo, but she finds Gemma's scent hypnotic. There's a lot about Gemma that TS notices, like how she lights up when she's running. The joy on her face when she's got possession of the ball. How she—

"Ah, Shaw?" Gemma waves her hand in front of TS's face.

"Oh, um, did you say something?" TS can't believe she was caught . . . daydreaming? That's not something TS allows herself to do, especially on the field.

Gemma throws her head back with a laugh. "Yeah, I was wondering if you're going to that party tomorrow night."

"No." Even though the Taylors have been talking nonstop about it all week.

A car honks in the parking lot and Gemma gives a wave to an older guy driving. “Too bad.” She starts jogging to the car but then turns around. “You know, even Alex Morgan knew how to take a day off every once in a while.” She gives TS a wink before running toward the car.

TS blinks after her. She gets her phone out and already can see the seven million emojis that are going to come after this. It’s going to become a whole thing. But Gemma has a point.

TS⚽: So that party . . . I’m in

Our Chat (The Taylors Version)

TAY🎉: IT'S OUR FIRST HIGH SCHOOL PARTY!

TAYLOR🐝: The first of many

TS⚽: I'm going to ask something, but don't make a big deal out of it, K

TAY🎉: Who US? We know how to PLAY IT COOL

TS⚽: Never mind

TAY🎉: COME ON, TS!

TAYLOR🐝: You know we won't let this go

TAY🎉: You DID start it, TS!

TS⚽: Be chill

TS⚽: Will someone do my hair

TAY🎉: AHHHHH!!!! YES! YES!

TAYLOR🐝: Someone's feeling 22!

TAY🎉: Come over early! I've got so many cute barrettes and clips! GAH! I'VE BEEN WAITING FOR THIS MOMENT MY ENTIRE LIFE!!!

TS⚽: 🙄

TAY🎉: You asked for it

TAY🎉: LITERALLY 😂

TEFFY📚: Can I wear the hat?

TAY🎉: THE HAT!

TAYLOR🐝: Aw, Teffy, of course 🤗

FIVE

You're On Your Own, Kid

From what Teffy has seen from movies and read in books, high school parties are supposed to be fun. Then why is she dreading it so much?

She tugs on the black fedora, hoping it'll give her the confidence the other Taylors have as they walk into the party. While Teffy is eyeing all the different ways she can make a great escape if she needs to.

"Are you sure it's okay that we're here?" Teffy asks. All she knows is that it's some sophomore guy named James's house. The Taylors are all spending the night at Tay's. When her dad dropped them off, he gave them a big lecture about not drinking and to call the second they want to be picked up. It took everything for Teffy to not remain in the safety of Mr. Johnson's car.

"Of course it's okay, the *lead singer* of the band personally invited me," Tay says with a flip of her curls.

"But what about the rest of us?"

"Please, you've got *the hat*, Teffy," Taylor says as she links their arms together. "Which automatically makes you the coolest person at this party."

"In the entire state!" Tay adds.

"Come on, people," TS says with a smirk. "It's *the world*."

They've got a point. The hat is the one they got from Mother herself when they went to the Eras Tour during fifth grade. Teffy still can't believe out of the entire Lucas Oil Stadium of nearly seventy thousand people, the Taylors were chosen to get the hat during "22," especially since they didn't even have tickets when they arrived. Teffy wraps her arms around herself, remembering Taylor Swift telling them—after giving the best hug that's ever been given in the history of hugs—to share the hat.

And share they have. It's passed around when one of them needs an extra boost of comfort or confidence: when Tay's grandmother died, when TS missed a goal and the team was out of a tournament, when Taylor got her tonsils out.

As Teffy walks around the living room filled with her classmates and unfamiliar faces, she feels silly that she needs the hat to simply exist at a party. But the Taylors never question or mock, that's why she loves them so much. They're allowed to simply be themselves.

Taylor scans the room. "I wonder where Hunter is?"

"Hunter? Who's *Hunter*? Have I heard that name before?" TS taps her chin with her finger.

Taylor grimaces. "Ha ha, TS, you're *so* funny."

"Thanks for noticing!" TS crosses her eyes. "I'm also, like, the most mature of the group."

Teffy can't help but let out a nervous laugh. Taylor has been *extra* this week about that senior. Sure, he's cute, but he's also, like, old, but Taylor gets annoyed if anybody says anything negative about him.

"Hey!" Tay says brightly, probably sensing that Mount Taylor could erupt at any moment. "Taylor, weren't you going to use tonight as an opportunity to talk to people about the issues they face?"

"Huh?" Taylor's head is craned in a different direction. No surprise who she's looking for.

"Your campaign for class president," Tay reminds her.

"Oh yeah, totally." Taylor looks down at her phone. "I'm going to see if Hunter's here, I'll be right back." Taylor disappears into the crowd that's gathered in the kitchen.

There's some loud guitar feedback that causes Teffy to cover her ears.

"Oh! Reece is getting ready!" Tay exclaims as she heads over to where the band is setting up.

Something catches TS's eye. "I'm going to talk to my teammates. You good, Teffy?"

If Teffy was nervous when they walked in, she's utterly terrified now. They haven't even been here for five minutes and the Taylors are already dispersing. Teffy didn't want to come here in the first place, and now she's supposed to . . . what? Just hang out by herself. Be comfortable around strangers.

"Teffy?" TS asks, her attention focused across the room. "You can come with."

"Oh, no, I'm okay," she lies. She doesn't want to keep TS from being with her team. Or Taylor from Hunter. Or Tay from listening to Reece's band.

Then what exactly is keeping Teffy here? Why is she here?

This was such a bad idea.

TS pauses for a moment. "You sure?"

Teffy isn't sure about any of this, but she doesn't want to hold her friends back. "No, I'm cool. I think I'm going to head outside." More like hide outside. Teffy suspected this might happen, so she had tucked a small notebook into the back of the black leggings she paired with an oversized red sweater. She always has something on her to write with in case she gets inspired. Or bored.

Teffy weaves between people who are louder, taller, more settled than her. She tries to maneuver between two groups of friends, when her shoulder is slammed by a tall guy.

"Sorry," she says, even though Taylor tells her to stop automatically apologizing, especially when something isn't her fault.

"Cool hat!" the guy says. He's got broad shoulders and is wearing Indiana Pacers gear head to toe. Before Teffy can realize what's happening, he takes off his baseball hat and removes Teffy's hat—*Taylor Swift's hat*—from her head. "I think this looks good on me. What do you think?" he asks his friends as they laugh along.

"Oh, you look so sophisticated," a petite girl with short bleach-blonde hair says before she grabs it and puts it on. "Although it's way better on me." She takes a selfie.

"I need that back," Teffy says in a small voice, but she's drowned out by the group of three guys and two girls yelling over one another. Each one taking their turn with the hat and selfies.

Teffy reaches up to grab it, but the tall Pacers guy holds it above his head. "Didn't anybody teach you about sharing? This looks sick on me."

"I, um . . ." This can't be happening. There's a sting behind Teffy's eyes. She can't lose the hat. It means too much to her and the Taylors. She wishes she could stand up for herself like Taylor, but moments like this make Teffy want to fold in on herself. "Can you . . ."

Teffy absolutely can't cry in the middle of a party, but her lip is starting to twitch.

"John, come on!" comes a voice from behind her. A voice Teffy knows as well as she knows Taylor Swift's. "Give Teffy her hat. *Now.*"

Teffy turns around to see Liam standing behind her. He hands Teffy the bag of Doritos he was holding, then reaches out to take the hat from John.

"Dude, we were just having fun," John defends himself with an eye roll.

"*Dude*, you were being a jerk." Liam gently places the hat back onto Teffy's head, before putting his arm around her. "Come on, Tefs, let's get some air." Liam guides Teffy to a spacious backyard with only a few people scattered around the lawn. "You okay?"

Teffy can only nod. She's too scared she'll start crying. But then she looks into Liam's dark eyes and that swirling feeling in her belly intensifies.

"Probably not the best way for you to start your freshman year." Liam grimaces. "Sorry about that."

"It's not your fault." Teffy looks down at the bag of Doritos in her hands and holds it out to Liam. He pops a few chips into his mouth.

Between bites, Liam starts firing off questions: "How's your first week? Any teachers you like, dislike, anybody I need to have a talking-to, besides those jerks inside? I need you to tell me everything since we're not doing dinner tomorrow night."

The last part throws Teffy off. "We're not?" This was news to her. The Bennetts and Yoons always have dinner together on Sundays, but the last two got canceled. They also go on summer vacation, but that didn't happen this year because her parents needed to stay and work on a big order at the store. The Little League wanted new uniforms and her parents' store, Harrison by Design, does all the custom lettering for the athletic teams.

"Yeah, my mom said something's going on with the store." He shrugs. "They seem pretty stressed about it all, to be honest."

Teffy's parents have been spending more time at the store, but she didn't think anything of it. While Teffy's parents run Harrison by Design, the Yoons were the ones who fronted the money to open the store. The Yoons have investments in a lot of the businesses downtown, and a lot more money than Teffy's family, but it's never been a problem.

"But that's boring grown-up stuff. How's the songwriting going?" Liam puts another big handful of Doritos into his mouth. Teffy always cracks up at how much Liam eats.

"It's been—" Teffy starts, but Liam's attention goes behind her.

"Hey, babe."

Just like that, Teffy's heart collapses.

"I've been looking everywhere for you!" Cat Sullivan strides over to Liam and puts her arms around him. She's wearing a light blue tank top and white jeans. "I should've known you'd be with Teffy."

"Hi, Cat," Teffy says quietly. She starts shifting on her feet. This party is getting worse by the second.

"Oh!" Cat coos. "I love the hat, it's *adorable*."

Teffy feels like a child next to Cat. Not just because Cat's tall and gorgeous and always put together. Okay, it's a lot of that. But maybe Teffy *is* a child. She had to wear a hat as a security blanket. She needed Liam to save her.

Liam wraps his arms around Cat, and Teffy wants the earth to swallow her up.

"Liam!" Cat squeals, and she starts brushing at her white jeans. "I can't believe you're eating Doritos when you know I'm wearing white!"

Liam replies by putting more chips in his mouth.

"You're the worst!" Cat says, but she's smiling like she doesn't really mind it. Cat grabs Liam's hand and starts pulling him toward the house. "Come inside. The whole gang has been looking for you."

"Be right there. Promise." Liam gives Cat a quick kiss and Teffy looks away. Once Cat is back inside the house, Liam leans in. "You going to be okay, Tefs?"

She doesn't want him to worry about her. To treat her like a little kid.

"Yeah, totally," she says, the waver in her voice as loud as a bell.

Liam pauses for a moment. "Well, I'll miss you at dinner tomorrow night."

"You're going to miss my mom's cooking," Teffy teases.

"I mean, I drool thinking of your mom's lasagna. In fact, I may use it as my inspiration for the poem I'm supposed to write for English." Liam puts his hand to his heart before he erupts in laughter. It's a sound Teffy loves almost as much as the acoustic guitar melody from "willow."

"LIAM!" comes Cat's voice from the house, which makes Teffy's shoulders tense worse than that awful guitar feedback from the band.

Liam rolls his eyes playfully before he starts to head back inside. He turns around for a second. "And for the record, Tefs, you don't need to hide out here. You've got this. You're Teffy Bennett and don't you ever forget it."

Liam disappears into the house as Teffy grabs her notebook and sits down on the grass to write.

She's suddenly feeling very inspired.

Taylor never minded being on the shorter side. It is, however, a problem when she's at a party looking for Hunter.

Where are you? she texts him. She doesn't want to be needy, but she's been looking forward to this party all week. She stressed over her outfit for days and finally settled on a black miniskirt paired with a white button-down shirt she tied at the waist and a blue denim jacket. Of course, she's wearing a red lip. Classic. Stylish. Mature.

Taylor can't wait to get some time with Hunter outside school. Not that she's complaining. He stops by her locker every morning and swings by at lunch. When she talks, Hunter leans in and really listens to her. Even though it's mostly her babbling about her classes and family, but he doesn't make fun of her. He asks her questions. He's interested in her. In Taylor's chaotic household, it's often hard to get anybody's attention, but Hunter makes her feel like she's the only one there. And she matters.

I was about to ask you the same thing, Hunter replies.

I'm in the kitchen

Um, I'm in the kitchen, followed by, You playing hard to get?

Please. Taylor should probably not be so obvious around him. She likes to think of herself as calm, cool, and collected, but with Hunter, she's a fumbling mess. She just likes him so much. He's gorgeous. He's so cool. He's like those guys Taylor Swift writes about—the good ones, obviously. Not the jerks who mess with her. Hunter is totally a "King Of My Heart" guy and not an "I Knew You Were Trouble" one.

But how could Hunter be in the kitchen? It's not that big. Taylor searches but doesn't see him anywhere. He'd be hard to miss. He's tall. Over six feet. He always seems to be surrounded by a group. Which isn't surprising, he's so charismatic. Who wouldn't want to be around him?

Taylor scans the room again, and then turns around and smacks right into Hannah Reed.

"Watch it!" Hannah growls at Taylor.

"Yeah!" Greta Lucca, Hannah's minion, says. They're wearing the same sequined jacket, Hannah in purple and Greta in blue. Taylor saw those jackets at the mall and couldn't believe how expensive they were. But that's Hannah. She has to have the newest and best version of everything—and rub your nose in it.

So Taylor does what she always does whenever Hannah is near her: turns around and ignores her.

"Who are you even looking for?" Hannah asks, since she has to make everything her business. "Let me guess, one of the Taylors." She snorts.

Taylor faces Hannah, a smile on her face. "Yeah, it'll be easy to find Teffy since she's wearing *the hat*."

Hannah's face pinches up in annoyance. She may have gotten to see the Eras Tour in both Amsterdam and Indianapolis, but she didn't get to watch it from the VIP section *or* get a hug from Mother.

"Well," Hannah starts, pulling her shoulders back. "I thought you'd like to know that *I'm* running for class president. So maybe you should just give up now."

Taylor lets out a laugh. "Oh, I think I can more than handle you. You know what money can't buy you, Hannah? A chance against me."

Taylor turns on her red canvas shoes and walks into the living room, wondering if Hunter could be there. She sees she's missed a text from him while dealing with Hannah.

You at Daisy's?

Who is Daisy? Suddenly, Taylor feels jealous of this girl. That Hunter is at her place.

James's. It's then that Taylor realizes she doesn't even know James's last name.

Ah, you're at the sophomore party, makes sense

Taylor groans aloud. Maybe she should try to get a ride to this other party.

Probably for the best, Hunter texts.

What does *that* mean?

Another text from Hunter comes through. Didn't want to have to share you

Taylor's spirits perk up. Hunter wants to spend time with her. Alone.

How about a date? Tuesday?

OMG. Hunter is asking her on a date! But a Tuesday? She doesn't know how her parents will feel about her going out during the week. It's not like she hasn't gone over to Tay's on a school night.

No, Taylor is in high school. She may be the baby of the family, but she's *not* a baby.

Sounds great, she replies, even though it sounds absolutely amazing.

Taylor has a date. With a gorgeous senior.

Fortunately, her very loud squeal is masked by the band starting up in the living room.

Every artist has to start somewhere. Tay loves watching videos of a thirteen-year-old Taylor Swift sharing her songs with her family in their house.

Now she's watching Reece tuning his guitar as his band—three other guys: another guitarist, bassist, and drummer—gets ready. She's both extremely jealous and excited to hear Reece perform.

Sure, it's only a couple dozen of their classmates gathered, but it's something. A start. As Reece strums the guitar like it's nothing, Tay wishes she would've stuck with guitar lessons. And piano lessons. She just didn't have the patience that learning an instrument requires. That's why she loves singing. She can do it anywhere, and she does: the shower, her bedroom, with her dad in the car, and with Teffy when she shares the songs she's always scribbling in her notebook.

Tay wishes Teffy realized how talented she is. And, of course, Tay's dream is to get Teffy to agree to do what Reece is doing now. Get up onstage and perform. It doesn't have to be a big thing. It can be like Taylor Swift's acoustic sets. Just Tay on the microphone, and Teffy on the piano or guitar.

"One, two, one, two," Reece says into the microphone. He flips his long black bangs from his eyes, and he strums his guitar a couple of times. He nods at the other guys and they start playing a loud rock song.

It's not really Tay's vibe. She's a proud pop princess, but she does make a note to start checking out alternative playlists on Spotify. She's been itching to hear Reece all week. She's spied a few of his lyrics in his notebook during bio. His handwriting is messy, like his hand can't keep up with the words swirling in his head.

As Reece opens his mouth to start to sing, Tay nearly holds her breath in anticipation. It's a surprisingly low, rich voice. It reminds her of the guy from The National who sings on the *evermore* album. Tay can't help but wonder how she and Reece would sound together. Tay's singing voice is very much like her speaking one: bright and clear.

Most of the room ignores the band, but Tay's not embarrassed to be right in front. As the song continues, she feels a pair of hands wrap around her waist. It's Taylor, a smile on her face as they sway back and forth to the song, which is a bit emo, but Tay doesn't mind.

"This is so much fun!" Taylor shouts over the music. "And, Tay, he's *cute*!"

Tay can't help but admit that Reece *is* cute. While her initial interest in Reece was because they share the same dream, as she's standing in front of him now, she really wishes he would notice her. Not just as his biology partner.

"Okay," Reece says into the mic, his eyes down on the floor. There's a confidence he has when he's performing that vanishes once he has to address the audience. It's almost as if he's a reluctant front man. "We're gonna do a cover now."

Wait, that song he was singing, with lyrics like *"the curve of your smile"* and *"heart shatters into splinters,"* was an original? Tay almost can't believe that Reece would write something with such emotion.

Tay likes that Reece is deep. That he feels things, unlike most of the boys—and let's face it, they're *boys*—in her class.

A boy with feelings who can play guitar and sing! When she first laid eyes on Reece, she didn't really think he was her type, but now . . .

Swoon!

"And this song goes out to someone," Reece adds before he plays the opening chords.

Tay may be making it up, but she swears he glanced at her. She is right in front of him, but still. She knows she shouldn't make assumptions—or get her hopes up—but she can't help it. She's a positive person! She spends so much of her time cheering for others, she should be able to hype herself up.

It's just Reece now, with his acoustic guitar, and the melody seems familiar.

As soon as he sings the first line, Tay is frozen, while Taylor screams next to her.

Reece is playing a Taylor Swift song. Not just any song, an acoustic version of "Blank Space," which is one of Tay's favorites. Okay, she has about fifty thousand favorite Taylor Swift songs, but this one is up there.

As the song nears the chorus—and Taylor and Tay are singing along like they're back at Lucas Oil Stadium—Reece glances right at Tay when he gets to the part about writing a name.

This song so has to be for her, right? After all, she *is* named after Taylor Swift.

The song ends and Taylor screams next to Tay. She grabs her in a hug. "Oh, he likes you! We both might have boyfriends! Can you believe it?"

No, Tay can't believe it. Tay loves watching fun rom-com movies and always dreamed about meeting her one true love and having a happily ever after. She would fantasize she'd meet someone by bumping into them at a coffee shop or something, but having her cute science partner turn into a brilliant musician, well, that's even better than fiction.

Everything is turning out way better than she could ever imagine.

It's the hair that TS first spots from across the room. It's become a lavender beacon, beckoning her. A light in the sea of TS's classmates.

Gemma's in a corner of the living room, laughing at something one of their teammates has said. TS can't help but be impressed. Gemma is new to Harrison, new to the country, yet she seems so at ease. A quiet confidence.

Gemma's eyes go from Shanti, their goalkeeper, straight to TS. Her lips curl into a knowing smile, like she expected TS would eventually show up. She raises her can of cherry Coke as TS approaches.

"Guess you're up for some fun, Shaw." Gemma pops a Cheeto into her mouth before she holds out a bag to TS.

Since TS got serious about sports—she's not joking about making the US Women's National Soccer Team—she's cut out any processed foods from her diet. She focuses on protein, fruit, vegetables, and whole grains before a game. By the way Gemma holds out the bag, it's almost like a dare.

TS has literally given blood, sweat, and tears for soccer. She deserves a little treat now and then. TS grabs a handful of Cheetos, and the second she eats one, she silently curses herself for ever giving up such delights. It's not like she doesn't need fuel for her workouts.

"I'm always up for some fun," TS replies.

Always up for some fun? Is that flirty or too cheesy? TS internally cringes.

"I like what you've done to your hair." Gemma reaches out and pulls at a long strand.

"Thanks," TS replies before shoving some more Cheetos in her mouth, afraid she'll say something silly. Again.

It's not like Tay didn't fret over TS's hair for eighteen hours. Okay, it was more like fifteen minutes, but it felt like forever to TS, who rarely sits still. Tay used some product to smooth down TS's hair, and her curls are more defined. She refused anything too . . . Tay. But Tay's pale pink knotted headband keeps most of the hair out of TS's face and she even borrowed one of Tay's light pink shirts with lace trim.

"I like *your* hair," TS admits.

"Thanks!" Gemma ruffles it. "A girl's gotta find her own ways to stand out."

What TS wants to tell her is that she'd stand out no matter her hair color, but she stays silent.

Gemma continues, "Think I'm going to change it up. Either blue or pink."

"Pink looks so good on you" comes out of TS's mouth before she can stop herself.

Gemma raises an eyebrow, while TS wants to die. Now Gemma knows that TS has looked at her online profile and gone through her photos to see the different changes in her hair.

"I mean . . ." TS mumbles, wondering how she can recover.

Gemma gets out her phone and TS wouldn't blame her if she's texting a parent to come pick her up because there's a stalker who is obsessed with her. She types for a second before TS's phone buzzes in her back pocket.

"Why don't we just make it official, yeah?" Gemma says as TS sees a notification that Gemma is following her. She leans in. "And just so you know, I like the bracelets you and your friends make."

Oh wow. *Wow.* This means that Gemma has also been looking at TS's profile. That she's also curious about her. That's what that means, right?

See, this is why TS has avoided things that make her self-conscious and unsure of herself. There's a reason they're called *crushes.* That's what her feelings for Gemma are doing to her self-esteem.

"I can make you a bracelet," TS offers because she wants to keep talking to Gemma. "Any requests?"

"Surprise me." Gemma takes a long sip of her soda, while TS's head continues to spin. "So, Shaw, what else are you into *besides* sport?"

"Oh, well." It's like TS can't think beyond soccer and basketball and track. She spies Tay and Taylor dancing along to the band. "My friends. The Taylors. We're really close."

"What else?" Gemma asks with a curious tilt of her head.

"Oh, um . . ." Great, now TS seems like the kind of person who only thinks about sports, which is . . . somewhat true.

"Well, I think we can do something about that." Gemma takes TS by the hand and leads her to the dance floor.

It's in this moment that TS totally gets cults. She'd mindlessly follow Gemma anywhere.

Our Chat (The Taylors Version)

TAY🎉: Week Two (Freshman Year Version) here we go!

TAYLOR🐝: AKA the week I start campaigning

TAY🎉: Poster-making party at my house for MADAME PRESIDENT

TS⚽: IN

TEFFY📚: We also need to make posters for TS's first game.

TS⚽: Awww, Teffy 🥰

TEFFY📚: I'll be there on the bleachers cheering you on.

TAY🎉: Taylors stick together 🫶

SIX
You Belong With Me

Teffy doesn't know why she assumed high school would be any different.

It's not as if she thought she'd be a changed person. More confident like TS. More energetic like Tay. More in control like Taylor. It's almost as if she's become less. Smaller. More self-conscious. Even quieter, as if that were possible.

What happened to that girl who was in cheerleading? Who danced in the front row during the Eras Tour?

It's not like Teffy *wants* to be in the spotlight.

She likes the quiet life. Sitting in her bedroom reading a book where the girl gets the guy. In a way, it's a safe life. If she doesn't get onstage, she won't be humiliated. Again. If she doesn't put her songs out in the world, she won't have to deal with criticism. If she doesn't put her heart on the line, it won't get broken.

The thing is . . . all the other Taylors have something. TS has soccer. Taylor is running for class president. Tay has cheer and singing. At least Teffy has her songs. She likes that Tay wants to perform them. As long as Teffy doesn't have to get onstage with her . . .

Although, there is a benefit of being the quiet one: You notice things. While Taylor and Tay have been loud about their crushes, Teffy noticed TS's glances at the new London girl.

Does anybody have suspicions about her own true feelings for Liam?

"Kids!" her mom calls from downstairs after school on Monday. "Come on down, your father and I need to talk to you."

Teffy walks out into the hallway and sees her brother, Charlie, in his usually messy hair and vintage rock tee (today it's the Beatles).

"Do you know what's going on?" Teffy asks.

Charlie simply shrugs. That's her brother, the king of everything he does—school, football—who walks around like he doesn't have a care in the world. It's possible Charlie's been home even less than their parents with football, work, his friends, and his girlfriend.

"'Sup," Charlie says as he plops down on the couch.

Teffy hesitantly sits down next to him. She notices their parents' worried faces. Their mother is wringing her hands, while their dad is pacing the small space near the coffee table. Something is definitely going on. Teffy thinks about what Liam said about there being problems at the store, which wasn't a surprise. When Harrison by Design first opened, they were busy with orders from the school district and local companies, all hiring her parents to design custom uniforms, shirts, bags . . . If it can be personalized, they did it. But then people started ordering online. Going for "cheaper" options.

"Okay." Their mom takes a steady breath, while Teffy braces for the worst. "We're going to need to tighten our spending. The store has been struggling." *Okay*, Teffy thinks, *this isn't that bad, you knew this*. "And our business partners have decided to pull out."

But that . . . *that* she wasn't expecting.

"What?" Charlie snaps out of his daze. "You mean the Yoons?"

"Yes." Their dad finally stops pacing. "There's more. We made a poor investment based on a tip we got from the Yoons, and, well . . . we lost a lot of money."

Teffy's throat starts to tighten. Sure, her family isn't rich, but they never *really* struggled. They go camping instead of staying in hotels. She gets most of her clothes from secondhand stores. But she likes the vintage look.

"What does that mean?" Charlie asks. Seeing her normally chill brother's cheeks get flushed makes Teffy even more anxious.

"It means we need to be extra careful about money," their mom says calmly, measuring her words. "We're looking at all our expenses. We're sadly going to have to let our part-time people go at the store, so it'll just be your father and me. We'll be working extra-long hours. We all need to be mindful of what we spend. We hate for this to fall on you, but, Charlie, try to get more hours at Ritter's if you can. And Teffy, sorry, sweetie, but we need to cut expenses and, well, you're already such an accomplished pianist and taught yourself guitar, so we were hoping . . ."

Her piano lessons.

"Oh." Teffy blinks for a moment. While she likes taking lessons, it's to the point where she prefers to fiddle around with the songs in her head rather than practice Mozart. But still. It was something she had. Her music. But she knows there's only one answer she can give. "That's fine. Um, I was thinking of applying for a job at By the Book." Even though Teffy has a feeling this is bigger than something that can be solved by getting an after-school job.

"That would be great." Her mom gives her a grateful smile. "We also need you both to get those grades up, since the college fund has—"

"What?" Charlie stands up.

Their dad holds his hands out. "Now, Charlie, we always knew college would be difficult to pay for, so it's important to get as many scholarships and as much financial aid as possible. If you spent more time studying than with your friends—"

"Oh, so this is *my* fault?" Charlie snaps. "I can only do so much during my senior year."

"Well, maybe you should've taken school more seriously, like your sister," her dad says.

"You mean not have a life."

Hey! Teffy wants to protest, but she knows right now she needs to not make waves.

"That's enough. Sit." Her father points at the couch, yet Charlie remains standing. "It's also best if we take some time away from the Yoons while we—"

"I'm done listening to this." Charlie storms out of the house.

Leaving Teffy blinking in his wake. She's trying to process everything her parents have told them. She's always known if she wants to go to college, she'd have to get loans and scholarships. But are her parents really going to let business get in the way of their friendship with the Yoons?

Teffy's mom sits next to her. "You okay, sweetheart?"

No, Teffy is *not* okay, but she doesn't want to add any more stress to her parents' life.

"Yeah," she lies. Her attention goes to the door Charlie slammed just a minute ago.

"It's going to be fine," her mom tells her, but Teffy's not convinced.

Teffy has a sudden urge to get out of the house. It's like the walls are closing in on her. Usually, she loves nothing more than curling up on the couch with a book and a blanket, but she needs to go somewhere to think. "I'm going for a walk."

"Oh." Her mom exchanges a look with their father. "Of course, take your time."

With a quick stop to her bedroom to grab her notebook, Teffy heads outside into the cool evening air. Teffy knows the only way she'll make sense of everything is to write a song. She finds comfort in her footsteps as she starts to come up with a beat. Usually, her songs are a little quieter—very *folklore*—but she's in the mood for an angry song. Something like "Look What You Made Me Do."

Teffy's feet carry her to the park down their street. She used to go every day after school with Charlie and their friends, waiting until their parents called them home. As the streetlights go on above her, she wraps her cardigan around herself and enters the park to find somewhere to sit and start writing.

Teffy assumed the park would be empty, but as she approaches a bench near the swings, she sees someone sitting there. She stops suddenly, realizing that she's by herself at night in a park. Teffy takes a step back, and a twig cracks under her boot.

The shadowy figure turns toward the noise, but as soon as she sees the profile, she instantly relaxes, realizing it's the person she most wants to talk to in this moment.

"Liam?" Teffy says his name like a question.

"Hey, Tefs." He scoots over on the bench to make room for her.

"What are you doing here?" She sits down next to him.

He sighs. "I just needed a break, you know?"

Oh, does she. "Same." She pauses, not sure how much to share with him. "My parents told me your parents are dropping out of the store. And about the bad investment."

"Wait. Your parents were involved in that, too?" It's like a wave of recognition sweeps over his face. "All I knew is that my parents have been having all these calls and talking about diversifying their income streams . . . whatever that means. But your family . . . This is all making sense. I was wondering why I hadn't seen your mom in a while." The Yoons' house is a second home to Teffy's family. If Teffy can't find her mom, she's usually over there. "Oh, Tefs. I'm so sorry. Your parents must be really upset."

"They are." Even though her parents said their families needed to take a break, Teffy couldn't imagine not having Liam in her life. Her parents didn't explicitly say she wasn't supposed to see Liam. He's one of her closest friends; they can't do that to her. More importantly, Teffy couldn't do that to herself.

"And how are you?" Liam leans forward, studying Teffy's face so intently, it causes her to look away.

"I'll be fine." It's not like Teffy has a choice. But she will be fine. She has her friends. She'll get a job. She'll do whatever she can to make life easier for her family.

"Ah." A smile spreads on Liam's face as he glances at Teffy's hand. "And you came here to write."

She looks at the notebook. "Yeah."

"I wish I had an outlet like that. Instead, I have people trying to tackle me." He picks at a hole in his worn-out jeans. "I love how focused you get when you're writing in your notebook. You also bite your lip when it looks like you're struggling for a word."

"I do?" Her hands automatically go up to her lips.

But *wait a second*, does this mean that Liam's been watching her?

Teffy, be real. There's a part of her that wants to write the most epic love song about Liam watching her, but she knows he doesn't see her *that* way. Liam thinks of her like a little sister.

"Yeah." Liam's leg starts bouncing. He closes his eyes and Teffy takes this moment to study his profile. Her glance lingers on his lips.

"So why are you out here?" she asks, wanting to push her family drama—and her growing feelings for Liam—out of her head. "Or did you get kicked out again for overloading the washing machine with soap?"

"That was one time!" Liam throws his head back. "And for the record, the floors were extra clean with all those bubbles that came out of the machine, which nobody gives me credit for. And, in my defense, I was told to wash my clothes. Just following orders." Liam gives a little salute.

"You somehow manage to get more food on your clothes than in your mouth."

"Hey, I'm an excitable eater, okay? Jeez, there's a reason napkins exist."

"Oh, so you *are* aware you can use a napkin? Could've fooled me," Teffy teases.

Liam turns to her and opens his mouth in mock horror. "How dare you." He bumps his shoulder against her, and Teffy feels a spark of electricity running through her body.

Liam's smile dissolves as he looks out at the swing set.

"You okay?" Teffy asks.

"Yeah, just a little nervous about Friday's game."

"Friday? I thought JV plays on Thursday." Teffy put the game on her calendar, as she wants to be there for Liam.

"JV does play on Thursday, but I made varsity."

"Oh my goodness, Liam!" Teffy's voice echoes in the park. "You're just a sophomore, oh wow."

Even in the dark, Teffy can see Liam's cheeks start to flush. "Yeah, well, I'm no TS, who made varsity as a *freshman*."

"Who among us is TS?" Teffy admits with a laugh. She's in awe of her friend's talent and work ethic. Teffy knows TS will crush every goal she sets for herself.

"No kidding, but I feel a lot of pressure."

Pressure. It's something Teffy is starting to feel more of. *I guess this is what it's like to grow up.*

"But you deserve it," she tells him. Memories from their summer trips start swirling in Teffy's mind. "You were running circles around both our dads and brothers when we played pickup games during our camping trips. Remember that time Charlie teased me for not having any athletic abilities—I have tripped over nothing more times than I can count—but you insisted you and I play against him and my dad and we won. Which we did, need I remind you, because *you* did everything. I just stood there, which honestly is my favorite kind of athletic activity."

Liam's dark eyes sparkle. "And need I remind *you* that you and Jae once entertained us by doing the dance from the 'Delicate' video and you've got some moves. You never should've given up cheerleading."

Teffy sticks her tongue out, which just makes Liam laugh more. "I can't believe you remember that." Teffy should be embarrassed, but she loved those moments sitting around a campfire with the Yoons. And also, she *can* dance. She now prefers to do it in the privacy of her room with a hairbrush she'll occasionally sing into.

"You're such a rock star." Liam bumps his knee with Teffy's.

Things with Liam have always been like this: Easy, fun, it just feels natural and right. *If only*... It's a phrase that's on constant repeat when Teffy's with Liam. If only he could stop seeing her as a little kid. If only he knew how much he means to her. *If only* . . .

"So," he continues. "When are you finally going to let me hear these new songs you've been writing? And when's the concert? You know I'll be in the front row."

Teffy cringes. "Yeah, that's not happening, after, well, you know . . ."

Liam looks genuinely confused. "Know what?"

Teffy can't believe he's pretending to not remember. Liam was *there*. He was among the *hundreds* of witnesses. "The talent show when I was in seventh grade." She can hardly get the words out.

"That?" Liam shakes his head with a sigh. "Come on, nobody remembers that! *I* had forgotten about it, and, as I've more than proven, I have a Wikipedia-like knowledge of all things Teffy Bennett."

Teffy looks down at the ground. Even now the memories of that first—and only—performance make tears burn behind her eyes.

Tay had convinced Teffy to sign up for the talent show. Teffy had written a new song, "We're Just Getting Started," which was a fun, upbeat song, very "22." She got caught up in Tay's excitement of being up onstage. Tay convinced Taylor and TS to sing backup to the infectious "woo-ooh-oooh" chorus. They even came up with a dance routine. Let that sink in. TS was willing to get up onstage to dance *and* sing to support Teffy. How could Teffy say no to that?

She didn't sleep the night before. She couldn't eat that morning or at lunch, which turned out to be a blessing, because her stomach was in knots. As the other acts went on, Teffy's nerves got worse and worse. Her hands were shaking. She felt a buzzing in her ears. She smiled numbly and simply shook her head through Tay's numerous pep talks. As they took the stage, Teffy had trouble walking. She stood to the side with her guitar as Tay introduced them and the song. There was applause and it was time for Teffy to start strumming the guitar.

Teffy had practiced the song so much, she was going to rely on muscle memory. She lifted her trembling, sweaty hand, and the second her guitar pick made contact with the string, it flung out of her hand and skittered across the floor. TS rushed over to pick it up and handed it back to Teffy. "You got this," she whispered in her ear.

The silence in the auditorium was deafening. Teffy willed herself to strum, to play, to do *something*. She tried one more time and hit the wrong chord. Laughter slowly started working its way through the audience, then came "GET OFF THE STAGE" being yelled by Hannah, who was clearly loving this moment. The teachers tried to get the audience under control, but Teffy burst into tears and then ran offstage and locked herself in a bathroom stall.

The Taylors tried to console her, but it was too late. Teffy made a total fool out of herself. For weeks—weeks!—people would say mean things like "We're still waiting for *you* to get started" or "Where's your pick?"

When she really thinks about it, it was in the aftermath of the talent show that she decided it was better to keep things to herself. Her music. Her thoughts. Her voice.

"Hey, Tefs," Liam says warmly as he wraps his arm around her now. "It's okay."

It's not until she feels the tears on her face that she realizes she's crying.

Again.

And in front of Liam.

Like a child. Teffy doubts Cat cries over a talent show from two years ago.

But there's also the feeling of Liam's arms. How much she wants him to hold her, but not to comfort her just as a friend. But because he loves her, too.

If only . . .

Which is *not* helping with the whole crying thing.

"I'm fine," Teffy lies as she wipes her tears away. "I'm being silly."

"No, you're not. And you don't have to perform. I know it's what Tay wants, so tell me, what do *you* want? What's *your* dream?" Liam leans in. As much as Teffy doesn't like attention, she doesn't mind when it's coming from him.

Teffy hasn't really talked much about what she wants. Do you really blame her? There's something about saying it aloud that makes it real. But she wants to share it with Liam. "I'd like to be a producer. To be the person behind the person. Like all those people who stand behind Taylor Swift when she gets her Grammys."

"You want to be someone's Jack Antonoff."

"Exactly!" See, Liam has always just gotten Teffy.

"Well, I know you, Tefs. And you're amazing at anything you set your mind to."

Liam's gaze lingers on Teffy and the quiet of the park envelops them. Suddenly, Teffy doesn't feel so embarrassed anymore. Her heart starts to beat extra fast. She nearly jumps out of her seat when Liam's phone rings. When he pulls his phone out of his pocket, Teffy can see it's Cat calling.

"I should take this. It'll just be a second." Liam gives her an apologetic look as he stands up and picks up the phone.

Even though Liam has walked to the other side of the swings, she can hear his voice. The lightness he had while talking to her is gone. "Cat, that's not what I meant . . . It was just a joke . . . I didn't . . . That's not . . ."

When Teffy thinks about all that she wants, it's literally right in front of her.

As much as it pains her, it's the reminder Teffy needs: Liam doesn't belong to her.

Our Chat (The Taylors Version)

TAY🎉: Good luck on your DATE, TAYLOR!!

TAYLOR🐝: I'm totally tripping

TAYLOR🐝: A DATE! With a cute senior!

TAYLOR🐝: And he's picking me up . . . IN A CAR!

TAY🎉: You're such a grown-up

TS⚽: Or being kidnapped 😱

TAYLOR🐝: TS!

TS⚽: When we doing your campaign posters Prez Perez

TAYLOR🐝: After MY DATE

TS⚽: You have a date? Haven't heard anything about it . . . 🙄

TAYLOR🐝: TS 😒

TEFFY📚: Have fun, be safe!

SEVEN

So It Goes . . .

Being the youngest means that Taylor spent most of her life witnessing her siblings go through firsts: lost teeth, days of school, dates, dances, licenses, college acceptance letters . . .

But today is a big first for Taylor: a date. With Hunter. And yes, she's been excited and has talked about it nonstop since he asked her out on Saturday. She knows she's been *a lot*, but she still can't believe that someone like Hunter—who is gorgeous and charming and amazing—wants to be with her!

Unfortunately, her parents aren't sharing her enthusiasm. They almost weren't going to let her go out with Hunter—can you believe it? But Taylor figured it was just the prep she needed for the freshman class president debate. So she sat down with her parents and made her argument: Yes, Hunter is older, but as the youngest kid, she grew up watching shows and reading books that her older siblings were into. It made her more mature. Of course, her dad's counterargument was that she still sleeps with the stuffed bunny her grandparents gave her when she was five. Taylor kept her cool—see, if that's not showing maturity, Taylor doesn't know what is! They came to an agreement: Taylor could go; however, her parents had to meet

Hunter first. This didn't shock Taylor since it's a rule in the Perez household: Her dad has to meet the date and subject them to his cringey dad jokes.

Taylor would've agreed to anything to get to go out with Hunter.

"Please don't embarrass me," Taylor begs her parents on Tuesday.

"Who, me?" her dad asks from the hallway, and then walks into the living room wearing a boat hat with fake long hair.

"Dad!" she calls out as she holds her head in her hands. "Take that off, now!"

Taylor always assumed she'd love being an "only" child, with her siblings out of the house, but that means all the attention—including horrifying Dad moments—is solely for her.

"Miguel!" Taylor's mom scolds her husband right as the doorbell rings. "And you wonder why the rest of them left the state."

Her dad takes off the wig and puts it in a drawer as Taylor goes to open the door. She smooths out her pink-and-white plaid skirt she paired with a simple white T-shirt. Cute and chic.

She opens the door to find Hunter looking even swoonier than she remembers. He's wearing a blue button-down shirt and khaki pants, and he's holding a bouquet of sunflowers. "Hey, Taylor, you look beautiful."

He thinks I'm beautiful. Taylor wishes she could write like Teffy, as she'd pen the most momentous love song about this very moment.

Then, to her horror, Taylor's dad pipes up. "Let me have a look at him!" He opens the door wide. "Ariana, break out the lie detector!"

"Dad!" Taylor hangs her head. She grabs Hunter by the hand as she leads him inside. "He's just joking. In fact, pretty much assume anything out of his mouth is . . . just . . . ignore him."

Hunter lets out a relaxed laugh before extending his hand. "Pleasure to meet you, Mr. Perez. I'm Hunter Brown. I don't blame you for being protective, your daughter deserves to be treated with respect. It's something I plan on doing, sir."

Taylor's dad pauses for a moment, while Taylor is already dreading what's going to come out of his mouth. He shakes Hunter's hand tightly, and his eyes narrow. "Why don't you have a seat so we can have a chat." In the blink of an eye, her father's joking demeanor vanishes. He studies Hunter with a frown on his face. Maybe Taylor should ask him to tell one of his awful jokes.

Hunter turns to Taylor's mom. "And these are for you, ma'am."

While Taylor assumed the flowers were for her, she loves how thoughtful Hunter is being. She may have told him her parents were hesitant about the date, so she appreciates how he's trying to win them over. He must really like her, to do all this. It makes *her* like him even more.

Taylor's mom puts her hands to her heart. "Oh, these are just beautiful. Thank you so much, Hunter. It's been ages since anybody has been thoughtful enough to get me flowers." Then she turns to Taylor's dad and playfully hits him on the shoulder.

"I'm going to have to ask you to leave, son," Taylor's dad says with a wink, but his demeanor is still rigid.

Taylor is a bundle of nerves, but Hunter seems relaxed as he sits down on the big couch in the living room, across from two armchairs. He pats the place next to him for Taylor to sit down, which she happily does.

"You have a beautiful house, Mrs. Perez," Hunter comments as he looks around the living room.

"Why, thank you!" Taylor's mom puts the sunflowers in a vase.

"Okay, let's cut to the chase," her dad says. "What are your intentions with my daughter?"

"Dad!" Taylor exclaims. The fake hair hat was less horrifying than this.

"Taylor, you're my daughter. My fourteen-year-old daughter. I'm obviously going to have issues with you being taken out by a seventeen-year-old. It's my job—my duty—to look after you."

The room is silent for a moment, then Hunter gives her dad a nod. "Yes, sir. I understand your concern. But please know, I was raised right. I know how to respect women. To be honest, when I first met Taylor, I had no idea she was a freshman."

Taylor knows this is a lie.

Her dad grimaces. "Yeah, well, I was a senior once. Granted, it was decades ago—we did have electricity, by the way—but I know how boys can be."

"You also raised boys," Taylor argues.

"I don't think that's helping your case as much as you think, Taylor," her dad says with a laugh.

"Miguel." Her mom shakes her head.

Hunter's focus goes to the photos on the fireplace. "I see you used to played football, sir. What position?"

And just like that, her dad launches into the same stories Taylor and her siblings have heard a million times. Taylor stays quiet, not wanting to interrupt. Hunter keeps her dad talking, and as he does, her dad starts to relax ever so slightly.

Hunter looks at his watch. "Oh goodness, I didn't realize the time. I had made a reservation and don't want to be late. I'd really like to take Taylor to dinner, with your permission, of course, Mr. Perez."

"Well . . ." Her dad clears his throat and Taylor can hardly breathe. She practically wills her father to say yes. "She is to be back by eight o'clock sharp. Not a second later. Have I made myself clear?"

Hunter stands up to shake her dad's hand. "Of course, sir."

"Because there are no guarantees of a second date, and should I mention that I know the sheriff?" Her dad stands up tall, even though Hunter's a few inches taller.

Hunter lets out an uncomfortable laugh. Taylor wants to tell him her dad's joking, but he's not.

"It was a pleasure to meet you, sir, and you, Mrs. Perez." Hunter extends his hand to her mom, but she gives him a big hug.

Well, at least he won over one of them.

"Sorry you had to deal with that," Taylor says as they make their way to Hunter's SUV. "They're just protective."

Hunter gives her the wide smile that makes Taylor's belly fill with butterflies. "As they should be. You deserve to be looked after, Taylor. And I plan to do just that."

Oh my goodness. Taylor has basically turned into the smiley emoji with hearts around her face.

"Ready?" he asks as he starts up the engine.

A loud, blaring guitar and a gravelly voice fills the car, drowning out what had been an incredibly romantic moment. Hunter turns down the volume slightly. "You know this song?"

Taylor shakes her head, which causes Hunter to laugh.

"I'll make you a playlist, got to get you away from that bubblegum stuff." He then turns down the street toward downtown.

Um, *bubblegum* sounds like an insult. Besides, Taylor Swift isn't bubblegum. Yeah, she's got some fun songs, but she also writes these deep lyrics and melancholy tunes. Taylor is going to make Hunter a playlist. If he's going to hang out with her, *he* needs an education in all things Taylor Swift.

Especially since she and Hunter are just getting started.

Taylor has always been happy with her life. But sitting across from Hunter at Fiore's, it's like a huge piece of it snaps into place. She can't believe she's lived this long without Hunter being in it.

The entire date has been like a dream. When she's with Hunter, everybody else disappears. She loves hearing his stories: about his family, his friends, his life before her. She wants to know every single detail of his life. How he broke his arm when he was eight because his sister's cat got caught in a tree. How he goes over to his grandparents' for dinner every Sunday. How he loves watching sports but doesn't have the coordination to play. How he wants to go into broadcast journalism.

"There's one thing I don't understand." Hunter takes a bite of his chicken parmesan.

"What's that?" Taylor asks, leaning in. She's transfixed by his every word.

"How have I lived in this town my entire life and never met you? You're extraordinary."

Taylor's heart skips a beat. "Me? Hunter, you're . . ." She doesn't want to scare him off, she's only known him for a week, but he's all she thinks about.

"I get it." Hunter sighs. "I'm not good enough for you."

"What?" Taylor says loudly, feeling all the eyes in the quiet restaurant on them. *Let them stare*, she thinks. She wants everybody in the world to know that she's with Hunter Brown. "No, Hunter, I . . ." Does she say it so soon? How could she keep it to herself? "I really like you."

Hunter smiles so broadly, Taylor knows she said the right thing.

"For the record, I really like you, too, Taylor." Hunter leans back in his seat. "So, what are we doing Saturday?"

Oh wow. Taylor can't believe he's already planning a second date with her. That he's using the word *we*.

Taylor leans forward. "I don't know, what are *we* going to do?"

♥♥♥♥

"Oh my goodness!" Taylor exclaims at lunch the next day. "I still can't believe how perfect it all was, like, how is this my life?" She realizes she hasn't taken a breath since she sat down, but she needed to tell the Taylors every single detail of the best date she's ever been on. Sure, it's her only date (so far!), but it was truly amazing. *Hunter* is amazing.

"Sounds like a dream!" Tay replies. At least she's been focused on Taylor the entire time. TS has been fixated on her lunch, and while Teffy is listening politely, she doesn't seem as happy for Taylor as she should be.

Why aren't her friends more excited for her?

Taylor can't help it and continues, "And then! We were walking back to his car, and my feet were hurting since I decided to wear my mom's wedges and I started to get blisters and Hunter gave me a piggyback ride. Like, people were looking at us, but we didn't care. We were laughing and it was so fun."

"Sounds it!" Tay is practically exploding with excitement. "Well, did he kiss you or not!"

"Tay!" Taylor looks around, even though she wants to scream to the entire school that Hunter Brown did, in fact, kiss her. "He did," Taylor admits quietly, at which Tay practically screams.

It was just a light kiss on the lips when they were at the stop sign before her house. Then he tucked a strand of her hair behind her ear.

It was perfect. She knows she keeps using that word, but that's what it was. It was all so *perfect*.

"I'm so jealous," Tay admits. "I'm going over to Reece's house tonight for our bio project, which isn't a date or anything, but I like him sooo much. I've been listening to 'Blank Space' on repeat since the party."

"And I can't wait to hear all about it," Taylor adds, since she wants to be supportive of her friends. Be a positive example for TS and Teffy, who have been oddly quiet. "Oh, I can't believe I forgot the best part, well, besides the kiss: I'm going to the lake this Saturday with his friends."

"Wait." TS finally perks up. So TS *has* been listening? Because it seemed she was only paying attention to her chicken wrap and not Taylor. "This Saturday? I've got my first game this Saturday."

"Oh." Taylor totally forgot, but she already made plans with Hunter. "Well, there are other games."

"I'll be there, TS," Teffy adds.

"We're cheering for the boys . . ." Tay grimaces as TS rolls her eyes.

"I promise I'll be at the next game," Taylor adds.

"You promised you'd be at *this* one," TS reminds her.

"Wait, Tay, I don't think the football teams play on Saturday," Teffy says, smartly interrupting what could be an ugly fight between TS and Taylor. Even though Taylor hasn't done anything wrong.

"Yes, but Saturday we're cheering for the boys' soccer—"

"Who aren't even good," TS adds.

"Well, yes, but they're playing on Saturday." Tay mouths "sorry" to TS.

"Everybody is so busy," Teffy remarks. "When are we going to get together to do Taylor's campaign posters?"

"We can do it Sunday," TS offers.

"No, Sunday is all about you and your birthday!" Tay sings with a little clap.

TS rolls her eyes. "I know, but we can do posters while we're hanging around the pool."

Taylor lets out a breath that causes her bangs to move. First, she'll never understand why TS doesn't make a bigger deal out of her birthday. Taylor loves a fuss and makes it a whole weeklong affair.

"Don't worry about the posters," Taylor says. She knows she has so much to do, but the election isn't for weeks. She has other things to focus on.

Because when Taylor thinks of her future, all she sees is Hunter.

Our Chat (The Taylors Version)

TAY🎉: I need an outfit that says I'm here to study, but also you're the one I want so DATE ME

TAYLOR🐝: You're cute no matter what! Maybe glasses? Show him you mean business

TS⚽: Yeah, you're there to "study"

TAY🎉: WE HAVE AN ASSIGNMENT DUE!!!!

TS⚽: Keep telling yourself that kid

TAY🎉: I'M TWO MONTHS OLDER THAN YOU TS!!

TS⚽: K grandma 👵 Good luck with your study DATE

TAY🎉: GAH!!!!

EIGHT
Paper Rings

Tay knows this isn't a *date* date with Reece. She does. Truly.

However, that doesn't mean she isn't going to dress up. She once heard her dad tell a colleague that you should dress for the job you want. Which is why she likes to be stage ready in cute, colorful outfits.

But this is a different type of audition: one of someone trying to win the heart of a poet.

Tay loves wearing colorful outfits. Most of her wardrobe is filled with pastels and sequins. She likes shiny things, but that doesn't mean she doesn't have a few black items. So Tay settles on a black tank top, black shorts, but with her pink Converse. Very hip, very cool, very Reece, but with a smidge of Tay.

Tay bikes over to Reece's, and she double-checks the address. She isn't sure what kind of house she thought Reece would live in, but when she sees a three-story, giant sandstone house taking up nearly the entire block, she's taken aback.

As she walks her bike up the long driveway, her nerves go into overdrive. Before she has a chance to ring the doorbell, a woman in a gray maid's uniform answers the door. "Miss Johnson?" she asks.

“Um, yeah?” Tay has never had anybody refer to her in such a formal manner. Should she bow or something?

“Reece is downstairs, please follow me.” The woman smiles warmly as Tay tries to pick her jaw up off the floor at the modern house with floor-to-ceiling windows, bright marble countertops, and hints of light blue mixed in with the mostly white and beige interiors. Not a single black item in sight.

She remembers how in awe the other Taylors were when they went to her house for the first time, but Reece doesn’t live in a house. It’s a mansion.

Music is coming from the basement and Tay goes down the stairs to a large room with the biggest TV Tay has ever seen in her life, along with every instrument imaginable, and a room off to the side with a microphone.

“Is that a recording studio?” Tay greets Reece, all manners escaping her.

Reece gives her a nod, shifting on his feet. Tay has noticed Reece has this jittery energy when she studies him—they were in class, after all. It’s not like Tay’s energy, where it’s because she’s excited—it’s like he’s nervous.

He can also be really quiet. It takes him a bit to warm up, which is okay since Tay never has trouble filling silence.

But sometimes she finds herself at a loss for words when she looks into those crystal-blue eyes. When his hair falls onto his face as he scribbles all his thoughts down. When his cheeks get flushed when he gets excited. How red his lips get.

Tay forces herself to look away from Reece, even though he's so cute.

"This studio is so cool! Have you recorded? Do you know how all these buttons work? Do the Archers practice here?" She also realizes she needs to stop talking to give Reece an opportunity to answer her.

Instead of replying, he gives her a bashful smile.

"Do you know Teffy Bennett?" Tay suddenly has visions of recording her debut album here, but with Teffy at the control board.

Reece simply shrugs in response.

"Oh, well, she's one of my best friends and I think I've mentioned before that she writes songs, too. I know she'd love to get her hands on this." Tay walks over to all the knobs and displays on the console.

"Cool," Reece finally replies. "You want something to drink?"

"I'm okay, thanks." She stops gawking at the basement and turns her attention back on Reece. "I brought you something." Now it's Tay's turn to feel nervous. She'll admit it's a bit silly, but last night when she was studying, she got the urge to make Reece a (maybe more than) friendship bracelet. Tay's entire arm is practically filled with the different ones she and the Taylors have made.

She pulls out the black-and-white beaded bracelet with THE ARCHERS spelled out, after the Taylor Swift song and Reece's band.

Tay hands it to Reece and there's a hint of a smile when he takes it. "Thanks." He puts it on next to the leather bracelet he always wears. Tay hopes he'll think of her when he sees it.

"So." Reece gives her a single nod. "We should get to studying."

"Oh yeah, of course." After all, that's why she's there. But she can't help but feel a little disappointed. She was hoping they'd get a chance to talk more since they aren't in class.

"'Cause I want to take you somewhere later," Reece adds as he opens his notebook.

Reece wants to take her somewhere! You know what that sounds like?

A DATE!

♥♥♥♥

"Need I remind you, it's a school night," her dad says when Tay calls him to ask if she can skip dinner. No matter how busy Tay's dad is with work, he always makes sure he's home in time for dinner.

"Dad," Tay says quietly, even though she excused herself to the enormous bathroom to call. "I've got this biology project, then we're going to grab a bite to eat at the Coffee Cave. You know how much I need help with bio."

What she doesn't tell him is that they already finished their project.

"Please, Daddy," she says sweetly.

"Tay . . ." he sighs.

"Pretty please with a zillion candy-coated hearts."

There's a pause, Tay is too scared to take a breath. "I'll be there to pick you up at eight sharp."

"Thank you! Thank you! You're the best!" Tay jumps up and down, knowing she'll have to play it cool when she gets out of the bathroom. She doesn't want to scare Reece off with her enthusiasm, which has been hard to contain since being with Reece makes Tay want to do backflips and roundoffs.

Tay really does try to be calm on the ride over—Tay on her bike, Reece on his skateboard with his guitar strapped to his back. The Coffee Cave is in the basement of a record store, and the name isn't a coincidence: It's dark with no windows and the wood-paneled walls are filled with graffiti. But Tay's focus is on the sign at the front: OPEN MIC TONIGHT.

"Open mic?" she asks, realizing that Reece brought her there to hear him sing.

He raises his eyebrows. "Yeah, let's see what you've got."

Wait. Reece wants *her* to perform? She's both excited and terrified. She loves performing, but usually it's for her dad and the Taylors and with Teffy beside her. And Reece is in a band; what if he doesn't think she's any good? Gah! But also, Tay has no idea what song she should sing. She wants to impress Reece, but she wouldn't feel right doing one of Teffy's songs without her, plus, she needs Teffy there on the piano or guitar. Should she message her and ask her to join them? Wait, no, she wants this to be just her and Reece. A date, right?

Before she can reply to Reece, he puts her name down.

Her mind continues to race on what song to sing. There's a small stage with an upright piano that's seen better days. "So, I can't play the piano or guitar and I prefer to sing with accompaniment."

Reece guides them to a table toward the front. "No worries, I can do it. What do you want to sing?"

Oh wow. Reece wants to be onstage with her! And she doesn't have to beg!

"Taylor Swift," Tay replies quickly because, obviously.

Reece nods for a moment. "Okay, what about 'exile.' I can play the piano and do the Bon Iver part."

"Oh, um . . ." Tay knows the lyrics, but she prefers to do more up-tempo songs as it hides any nerves she has. But the thought of singing that song with Reece is too good to pass up. "We haven't practiced, though."

"I'm not worried," Reece says with the cool confidence that Tay notices he only has when it comes to performing.

"Okay, me neither," Tay lies. "Do you ever get nervous when you perform?" Tay can't help but think of the last time she was on a proper stage, with poor Teffy.

Reece plays with his leather bracelet. "When I play, no. When I have to talk, yeah."

That's not surprising since Tay does most of the talking when they're together.

"Well, I can talk for both of us."

Reece gives her a smile, and Tay's stomach does a little somersault that has nothing to do with going up onstage.

She waits patiently as a couple other people go first—one guy reading slam poetry, another woman singing some Broadway song. Then her name is called, and Reece heads to the piano.

Reece begins the moody intro and then starts singing. His low voice causes Tay's heart to beat even faster. She's so enamored by watching him perform, she almost misses her part. She closes her eyes and begins her verse, which is fitting since she can practically feel Reece's eyes on her. While "exile" is about two exes running into each other, in that moment, with their voices blending, Tay can only feel like this is the start of something.

A very big something.

Our Chat (The Taylors Version)

TAY🎉: HAPPY SATURDAY!!!

TAYLOR🐝: It's SO nice out, perfect for a day at the lake

TAY🎉: With your BOYFRIEND

TAYLOR🐝: Stop

TAY🎉: You LOVE it!

TAYLOR🐝: I doooo! I want to tell him all my hopes and dreams

TAY🎉: AND KISS HIM 😘😘😘

TAYLOR🐝: Yes, yes, yes!!!

NINE
Stay Stay Stay

Taylor knows this is big. Hunter wants to not only spend the whole day with her but for her to meet his friends.

He hasn't officially asked her to be his girlfriend, but she's not sure how this works. Is it too soon? Should she ask him? Is that needy? Or worse, childish?

The doorbell rings and she forces herself to count to ten before she opens the door. She'd been watching the road from her bedroom window and saw Hunter pull up. She's grateful her parents aren't home so Hunter doesn't have to deal with them. They sat her down this morning and gave her a lecture about drinking and consent, and, like, it's just a day out at the lake.

"Hi!" Her smile is so big, she can't believe her face hasn't cracked open. Hunter makes her *so* happy.

"Hi to you." Hunter then pulls Taylor by the waist and gives her a full kiss on the lips. Her knees go weak. There's a tingling through her body.

Yeah, today's going to be a good day.

Hunter pulls away and brushes her cheek with his thumb. How is it even possible Taylor is still standing? *Swoon!* "You ready?"

"Yes!" She points to the beach bag she packed for today. "I have some chips and soda. And something for you!" Taylor hands Hunter a bracelet she made with red and white beads with his name. She hopes it's not too childish, but she noticed a lot of the people he sits with have bracelets.

"Aw, I love it!" He slips on the bracelet and gives her another kiss. "Thank you."

Taylor really wants to make herself another one and wear it since it feels as if Hunter's name is already on her heart.

Hunter looks down at her outfit. "Is that what you're going to wear?"

"Oh, um, yes?" Taylor's wearing her Eras Tour T-shirt with a pair of relaxed boyfriend jeans. She assumed it was a casual day at the beach, so she wanted to be comfortable. "Should I change?"

"I mean, you look amazing no matter what you're in, but you might want to wear something more . . . grown-up." Hunter takes her by the hand and gives it a little kiss.

"Right. Okay. I'll be right back!" Taylor says brightly, not letting on how embarrassed she is that she totally got her outfit wrong. She runs up to her closet and thinks about the outfits the girls wear who sit at Hunter's lunch table. She grabs her sister's old lace top and a denim miniskirt. She may be a bit cold, but that's what Hunter's for, right?

Taylor is so grateful Hunter told her to change before she made a total fool out of herself in front of his friends. She doesn't want to make any false steps today.

"Better?" Taylor asks as she arrives back downstairs.

By the smile on Hunter's face, she knows she made the right choice. "Perfection, as always."

"Great!" She goes to grab her beach bag, but Hunter beats her to it.

"Allow me." Hunter picks up the bag and carries it to his SUV. He even opens the door for her. Taylor can't believe her luck to find someone so kind . . . and also super gorgeous. *And* what a gentleman!

As they ride out of town, Taylor sees the soccer field where TS will be playing in a couple hours. The day before her birthday, no less. Guilt floods her. She's been to every one of TS's matches since they met. Taylor knows how important soccer is to TS and she feels like she let her down in some way.

"Everything okay?" Hunter glances at her.

"Yeah, um, what time do we need to meet your friends? Maybe we can be a little late?"

Hunter pulls the car over to the side of the road and shuts off the engine. He turns so his full attention is on her. "Okay, let's talk. What's up?"

"Nothing." She doesn't want to be a pain. He made these plans and now she's trying to change them.

"Are you sure? It seems like something."

"It's just . . . TS is playing today, and I feel like a bad friend for not being there."

Taylor wasn't sure what Hunter's response was going to be, but him bursting out in laughter wasn't it. "Sorry, babe. You're so cute when you're upset."

“I’m not upset,” Taylor says. She’s not sure what she’s feeling. But she likes when Hunter calls her *babe*. It’s waaaay better than being called a baby.

“Listen, you can go to the game if you want. It’s just, I really like hanging out with you and I want you to meet my friends. I want you to be part of my life.” He places his hand on her bare leg, and she hopes he doesn’t notice the goose bumps that have just erupted from his touch.

“No, I want to go. I want to meet your friends and be with you.” She realizes she’s being silly. It’s just one game and TS will understand. Taylor will make sure to be at the next one.

“That’s my girl.” Hunter places his hand on Taylor’s cheek and draws her in for a kiss. It’s just as sweet as the five—and yes, Taylor’s counting—they’ve exchanged so far.

Hunter pulls away and gives her a tender kiss on the forehead. “Let’s go, I made a playlist for the drive.”

A half hour later of loud rock and rap music that Taylor really isn’t a fan of, they arrive at Windermere Lake Park. They walk through a path surrounded by trees, then they come to a clearing near a lake house and pier.

“About time, dude!” comes from a guy Taylor recognizes from her older brother Anthony’s former baseball team. “Hey, you’re Tony’s little sis, right?”

“Yeah, hi, I’m Taylor!” Taylor pulls her shoulders back, trying to exude the same cool confidence as the other girls hanging around a picnic bench. Even though she doesn't want to be seen as little. She doesn't want Hunter to think she's too young. First, her clothes, and now this. "I brought some soda and chips!"

"Soda." The guy laughs. *Why is soda funny?* "That's cute." *And how is it cute?*

"I'll get you a drink, you want a Coke?" Hunter asks.

Taylor nods and notices the older girls exchanging looks and whispering to one another, all while staring at Taylor.

"Be right back!" Hunter jogs over to the table. He puts the different sodas she brought into a cooler, then pulls out a can of Coke for her.

It takes everything for Taylor's face to remain neutral as she watches Hunter being handed something in a small glass and he downs it all in one go, wincing as he does it.

Taylor had such high hopes for today, but now she's incredibly uncomfortable. She doesn't know anybody here, except Hunter.

A voice in the back of her head starts whispering to her, *You shouldn't be here. You should be at TS's game. With your friends. That's where you belong. Not here.*

It doesn't really matter since she has no way to get to TS's game. Or home. She doesn't want to ask Hunter to leave and make a scene with his friends. They'll definitely think she's a baby.

Hunter comes back with a smile on his face. He holds out the can of Coke with a bow. "The finest of carbonated beverages for the lady."

Taylor gives him a smile, but Hunter can tell something's wrong. "Hey, you okay?"

"Um, yeah." Even though she isn't. Taylor doesn't want to say it, but something about being here doesn't sit right with her. "Maybe I should go."

"No, you gotta stay with me." Hunter leans down so she can look into his pale hazel eyes. "You trust me, right?"

She nods. Because she does. She knows Hunter will look out for her. He wouldn't do anything to make her uncomfortable.

She's sure it'll be fine.

Our Chat (The Taylors Version)

TAY🎉: GOOD LUCK TODAY, TS! Wish I was there to watch you START!!

TAYLOR🐝: Are you going to score a zillion goals, TS the STARTER?

TS⚽: that's how soccer works

TAY🎉: CHEER FOR ALL OF US, TEFFY! 🎉🎉🎉

TEFFY📚: On it.

TS⚽: Thanks Taylors 🥰

TEFFY📚: Just get your expectations in order. We know I'm no Tay.

TAY🎉: WHO IS?

TAYLOR🐝: Can you imagine TWO Tays?

TS⚽: 4 of us is enough

TAYLOR🐝: Can you really have enough of our awesomeness?

TAY🎉: NEVER

TEN
How You Get The Girl

It's go time for TS.

She lives for game days. They start out the same way: waking up to her specialized alarm to the synth beginning of ". . . Ready For It?" She does a quick ten-minute stretch before jumping into a shower, followed by a breakfast of cheesy scrambled eggs, a bagel, an apple, and a protein shake. She keeps her headphones on during the ride over to the game while watching key moments from the US Women's National Soccer Team. TS especially likes when Alex Morgan scores with a header with only thirty seconds left in the 2012 Olympic semifinals to lead USWNT to victory. It shows that a game can turn around at any moment.

Sort of like life.

All her hard work has paid off. TS is *starting* as a freshman on the varsity team. She pretended to not be shocked when Coach told her at practice yesterday. She went home and did a group video call with the Taylors and they all danced around to "Cruel Summer" since they love singing—oh, who are they kidding—*screaming* along to the bridge.

TS did it. And she's not going to let anything get in her way until they win state and she gets noticed by the national team.

TS's headphones remain on in the locker room. She listens to a special Taylor Swift mix made by the Taylors with all their favorite "hype songs." Tay picked "Shake It Off," Taylor's is "22," and Teffy's oddly is "I Can Do It With a Broken Heart." Which does have a nice beat and proves that no matter what's thrown at TS, she won't let anything distract her on the field.

There's a tap on her shoulder, and TS finds Gemma standing in front of her. She removes her headphones. "Hey."

"Am I interrupting some special pregame ritual?" Gemma asks like it's a joke, but she sort of is.

"I like my routines," TS admits. She doesn't return the smile since she's in game mode.

"I love how focused you are. Well, I don't want to bother you, but thanks again for this." She holds up her arm to show the GEMMA 18 bracelet TS made with the blue-and-gold school colors and Gemma's number.

"Same, TS!" Shanti holds up her bracelet.

TS decided to make them for everybody. Team spirit and all that.

"You're welcome." TS looks down at her TS 13 bracelet.

"Well, let's start the season off right, yeah?" Gemma holds her hand up.

"Yeah." TS gives her a high five before going back to her routine, pushing down those butterflies.

When it's time to take the field, TS pictures what it must be like to walk into a packed stadium filled with fans. She once took the Taylors to see the Indy Eleven Women's Team. They were four among the crowd of thousands, but this is Harrison High. Her team walks out to tepid applause from the dozens or so people in the stands. TS's parents are sitting next to Teffy, whose nose is buried in a book. But, hey, at least she's there.

"Let's go, team!" Coach Callahan brings them all into the center. "We've been practicing for this moment. Hustle. Don't give them any opportunities to score. 'Team' on three."

TS puts her hand in the center, and even though there are over twenty other hands in the pile, it's Gemma's that's right on top of hers. They break away and TS puts her game face on. She tightens her ponytail and takes the field. Whenever she's in the middle of a game, she has this intense focus. She never lets the ball get far away from her, but she can also sense the other players: their positions, even their next moves.

As the game starts, TS isn't surprised Gemma keeps up with her. They make a great team. Gemma assists TS in the first goal of the year. *The first goal*. Which TS made as a *freshman*. For *varsity*! While TS has a tiny internal celebration, it's short-lived when the Springfield Ravens score shortly after and they go into the half tied.

While her teammates are stressed during the half, TS remains calm. Okay, so she's internally freaking out from scoring and them being tied and also Gemma is sitting *right* next to her, but TS needs to show maturity and leadership qualities so she'll be captain next year. It's all part of her plan.

Gemma nudges her. "Brilliant game so far, but that one forward is fast."

"Yeah, but she always slows down in the second half." TS knows the Ravens are a better first-half team. She's studied the tapes. They don't have the conditioning that TS has been training for all summer. "We got this."

"Maybe let me score this time?" Gemma gives TS a wink.

"Just try to keep up," TS teases . . . and nearly winks back, but then stops herself. She shouldn't be . . . Is Gemma flirting? Or is this just team talk?

TS shakes her head, as she needs to keep her focus on the second half.

"You know, you're allowed to have fun out there, yeah?" Gemma says playfully. She then scowls, which TS thinks is an imitation of her. "You're so intense."

"Oh, well . . . I want to win." TS doesn't come into a game wanting to lose or tie. She's here to win and that takes concentration. TS puts her headphones back on for the last couple minutes of the half to get back into that focused mind frame.

Game, game, game.

But then *Gemma, Gemma, Gemma* pops into her head.

TS shakes it off. Once she hits the field, she's back to the intensity that Coach Callahan and her teammates expect from her. What *she* expects from herself. TS sees Gemma open and does what Gemma asked and passes the ball over to her . . . and Gemma scores! With only five minutes remaining, the Eagles pull ahead.

We so got this.

TS doesn't slow down or hesitate until that final whistle blows. And when it does, she jumps and pumps her fist into the air. Gemma comes running over and throws her arms around TS. Which may top the feeling of winning. Winning is something TS has become used to; *this*, with Gemma, however . . . that's new.

"Thanks for the assist, mate!" Gemma wipes the sweat from her forehead. "I thought I was going to have to wait forever and ever to finally score."

With the win secured, *now* TS can let loose and have fun.

"Well, I figured I owed you one," TS replies, impressed she was able to come up with a somewhat decent comeback. Although TS needs to work on her *game* game.

"Pizza after?" Gemma asks, and TS nods, even though she wasn't aware the team was planning on going out, but that's what she gets for keeping her headphones on while the team chats.

"Cool!" Gemma gives TS one more hug, before she sprints over to her parents.

TS jogs over to Teffy, who has been standing over on the sidelines. "Hey! Thanks for coming!"

"Of course!" Then Teffy pulls out a bag of orange slices. "It's still Charlie's favorite postgame snack."

"Teffy, you're the best, for real." TS bites into a perfectly juicy section. "Seriously, it means a lot that you're here for me."

"Forever and always."

TS tilts her head, trying to get a read on Teffy. She's been unusually quiet the past week. "And, for the record, if you ever played somewhere, I'd be there cheering you on."

"You know that's not my style, but I have been writing a lot lately. I have a couple songs that I've been trying to share with Tay, but she's been so busy," Teffy admits with a frown.

"Well, I can't wait to hear them." TS means it. Teffy's songs are really good: The melodies are as sweet as she is, but the lyrics give an insight into her that she usually doesn't share. "All good?"

Teffy nods for a moment, then looks down the field. "Yeah, things with my parents are a bit tense at home. The Yoons are getting out of the store and my parents have been really stressed."

"Oh, I had no idea." TS puts her arm around her friend. "That's got to be tough, I know how close you are with Liam."

Teffy grimaces for a moment, then simply shrugs.

Huh. TS can tell there's something there. But she also knows when someone isn't ready to admit something. But no matter what, TS will be ready for Teffy whenever she's willing to share. "Just know I got you."

"I do." Teffy looks over her shoulder and gives a little wave. TS turns around to find Gemma standing there, with jeans on and a Chelsea football shirt.

"Oh, we're going for pizza, want to join?"

Teffy shakes her head. "I'm good, but you have fun." She goes to leave, but then turns around. "And just so you know, I think Gemma is really cool. You two make a good team." Teffy gives TS that smile of hers that means she really is happy for someone.

"Thanks, Teffy." TS hugs her again before she leaves.

But there's this scratching at the back of TS's mind as she takes a shower. What exactly did Teffy mean by the Gemma comment? Has TS been *that* obvious? Should she be embarrassed? Or worse, does Gemma know?

Once she gets out of the locker room, TS notices that most of her teammates have left.

"Hey!" she says to Gemma, who is sitting on the team bench. "Where are we meeting everybody?"

Gemma tousles her lavender hair. "Nope, just the two of us. Cool?"

Cool? Is it cool?

TS somehow manages to squeak out an "Oh yeah, sure."

But in fact, it sounds pretty awesome.

Nothing stirs up TS's appetite like a win.

"We should get the cheesy bread, yeah?" Gemma asks as they sit across from each other in a booth at Galleria. "My mum got delivery here the other night after she nearly gave us food poisoning since you lot use Fahrenheit instead of Celsius. She basically tried to roast a chicken on the lowest setting." Gemma lets out a loud laugh at the memory.

"Has it been hard adjusting?" TS has lived in Indiana her entire life.

Gemma shrugs. "A little, just certain things you all say and do.

Like, we say 'football,' not 'soccer,' since, you know, we play with our *feet*, unlike your American football. That's going to take me a bit to get used to. The one that keeps getting me is 'pants' for us is underwear. What you call 'pants' is trousers. So on my first day when someone complimented my pants, I thought my actual pants were showing!" Gemma's big green eyes go wide. "Now, *that* would be a way to make a first impression, for worse or for better."

Had TS known she and Gemma were going to do something, she would've packed more than gray sweats to wear after the game. She'd like to make a good impression on her. Although, TS has never been one to really fuss over clothes; she likes comfort. There's something about Gemma that makes TS a little uncomfortable, but in a new-feeling way. Not in an I'm-not-liking-this way.

"Well, I really like your accent," TS admits. British people just sound more sophisticated to TS.

It isn't lost on TS that even Taylor Swift has dated a few Brits.

"Okay, let's try it out." Gemma leans across the booth. "Say, you what, mate?" But the way Gemma pronounces the words, it sounds more like *you* wot, *mate?* It has more of a rougher accent. "Or, you a'right, babes?"

TS tries to repeat it, but she keeps tripping over the different pronunciation. Gemma giggles as she repeats, "You a'right, babes."

"Baaaybes," TS tries, which she purposely gets wrong because she likes how much Gemma laughs at her poor attempt at a British accent. "Okay, you try speaking like an American. Repeat after me."

"Oh, okay." Gemma sits up straight, her entire focus on TS. "Teach me your American ways."

"Hey, how you doin'?" TS says in more of a New York accent than her plain Midwestern one.

"How YOU doin'?" Gemma does a spot-on impression of some New York mobster, which causes TS to let out a very loud laugh that is way more Tay than her.

And she's not mad about it.

"So, spill on all the Taylors you hang out with?" Gemma starts. "Is that even your real names or are you in, like, a cult?"

"We are in the cult of Taylor Swift," TS says.

"Where do I sign up? I can be London *Girl*! And if you need to check my credentials, I saw her at Wembley Stadium on her last night of the Eras Tour. We not only got the surprise performance of 'Florida!!!' with Florence, we—"

"Got the acoustic set with Jack!" TS remembers watching the live stream and screaming when Taylor floored everybody by inserting a new song into the *Tortured Poets* set.

"I know! I can't believe my luck. My life hasn't been the same since that epic show." Gemma takes a huge bite of cheesy bread.

"Same." TS is going to say the next sentence slowly as she wants to take in every reaction that will surely cross Gemma's face, which is an open book. Even when they're on the field, Gemma doesn't hide when she's frustrated, but usually she's smiling. Like she is at TS right now. TS can't wait to watch that smile get even bigger.

"So, the Taylors and I were the ones who got the hat when—"

"YOU GOT THE HAT!" Gemma screams out in the pizza place. Her mouth has dropped open, her cheeks are getting flushed. "Oh my goodness! I remembering seeing that video! You were one of the four girls! THE TAYLORS!" It starts coming together in her mind. "Oh wow. Just wow. I've never been seething with such jealousy. Where is it? I must see it! Can I touch it? Can I *wear* it?"

"Why, so you can steal it?" TS jokes, although she and the Taylors are super protective of the hat. It's on a rotating schedule, and whenever it's at TS's house, she checks on it constantly like it's a pet. She would never forgive herself if anything happened to *the* hat.

"Never! It would be like going to visit the Crown Jewels. Just to admire it. Besides, I want to hang with the Taylors. I have Spanish with Teffy, but she doesn't really talk much in class. So, is there some sort of initiation? Do you need me to take a test?"

TS can see Gemma fitting in with her friends. "Oh, nothing like that. Just a little blood sacrifice," TS jokes.

"Well, if your friends are anything like you, it would be worth it."

TS blushes at the compliment. But does that mean she wants to be just friends?

See, this is why TS never really thought much about relationships. It's too confusing and filled with drama, at least with what she's witnessed with her brother and sister: the crying, the yelling, the moping around. TS has never put herself in a vulnerable position.

Then again, two years ago TS broke her finger during a nasty collision on the soccer field. And it healed. So if her heart breaks, she guesses it could also be put back together.

All she does know is that she likes being with Gemma and doesn't want to let this feeling go.

"We are pretty amazing," TS admits.

"No doubt." Gemma pauses for a minute. She looks down at the table, but then glances up at TS between her pale eyelashes. "And just so you know, I like my American girls and eating pizza in the afternoon."

Oh my goodness, Gemma remade the "London Boy" lyrics about . . . TS?

Because while TS doesn't know all the ins and outs of dating, she definitely fancies this London Girl.

Our Chat (The Taylors Version)

TEFFY📚: No surprise, our TS was AMAZING today! One goal and one assist! Hope the rest of you are having a great Saturday!

TAYLOR🐝: Having a blast eating lunch down by the lake

TEFFY📚: Enjoy!

ELEVEN
invisible string

Teffy's bored.

It's Saturday night. She's in high school. Shouldn't she be doing more than finishing up her homework? Instead, she's trying to not get upset that the Taylors are all busy with their own things. Even her parents are spending the night at the store, doing inventory. She picks up her guitar and starts strumming.

She's been working on this one song, "The Secret of Us," for a while. She pictures Tay singing it. But there's a part of her worried that everybody will be able to tell it's about Liam, with lyrics like "*together since we were young*" and "*watch you grow along with my feelings.*"

Like a lighthouse signaling a ship to come home, there's a flash of lights across the room. She spies Liam waving to her. He holds up the whiteboard: *Park?*

Teffy nods. Guess she's not the only one without plans. And the fact that Liam wants to spend his Saturday night with her? It's not like they haven't spent countless weekends together, but ever since the spring, when Liam started dating Cat, he's been . . . preoccupied. Teffy puts on her favorite cable-knit wool cardigan, perfect for the cool August evening air.

Liam meets her on the far corner from their houses. He's got a light gray jacket covering a teal polo shirt. "Hey, Tefs."

"Hey!" She greets him with a hug. "You were great last night."

Liam grimaces. "We lost."

"Yeah, well, you had the longest return of the evening."

Liam glances at Teffy with respect. Teffy isn't the biggest sports fan, but she googled a few things before watching both Liam and TS play. And she also read the local paper's coverage. She zoomed in on the picture of Liam running with a ball. She almost printed it out.

"Plus, it's only your first game." Teffy wraps her arms around herself as they stroll to the park.

"Yeah, but to be honest, I'm sort of burned out on talking about football all day," Liam admits.

"Oh, okay." And because it's an itch Teffy wants to scratch, she asks, "Is that why you're not out with . . . your friends?" Teffy doesn't want to bring up Cat. She's nice and all, and really pretty in that totally put-together way, but she seems too . . . exacting for Liam. Cat is neat, tidy, controlled, while Liam with his room and hair and eating is all chaos. But in a good way.

"Yeah, I just wanted to have a chill night."

Teffy notices Liam also didn't mention Cat.

"Well, anyways," Liam says as he bumps Teffy playfully on the hip. "What's going on in Teffyland?"

"I applied for a job at By the Book." She doesn't share the reason why, mostly because Liam probably already knows.

"That's the perfect job for you."

"Right?" Teffy has been going to By the Book since she can remember. The store owner often holds new books that she knows Teffy will like. "Unfortunately, they're not hiring, but maybe closer to the holiday season." For now, Teffy is going to try to get more babysitting gigs.

"That's too bad." Liam seems to be fighting a smile. "So, um, I like that song you're working on."

Teffy stops in her tracks. "You never told me that you can hear me play!" She punches him lightly on the shoulder.

She is beyond horrified. Not just because Liam is listening to an unfinished song, but that he could hear the lyrics.

Liam looks down at the ground and kicks at a rock. "Yeah, well, if both of our windows are open, I can, just barely. You've got nothing to worry about, it's already my new favorite song. You have to play it for me for real."

There is absolutely no way Teffy can play "The Secret of Us" for Liam; he'd be able to see right through her.

But maybe that wouldn't be such a bad thing comes a voice from inside Teffy. The other Taylors are putting themselves out there: Taylor is with Hunter at the lake, Tay is at Reece's band rehearsal, and TS is having pizza with Gemma.

When she and Liam make it to the edge of the park, Teffy takes a long inhale of the crisp air. She can't wait for fall, it's her favorite season. As they start making their way on the green grass, she wills the leaves to turn golden.

Liam gestures toward the swings. "This may sound silly, but do you want to go on the swings? Remember when we'd spend all day here with Jae? You two would sing Taylor Swift songs."

Yes, there was a time when Teffy loved singing. Maybe it's before she realized that she didn't have the best voice. She wishes she could be as free as she was back at the Eras Tour, where the four Taylors sang their hearts out. Teffy didn't care if she didn't have the strongest voice. She was free.

"Any requests?" she asks bravely as they sit down. The song "You Belong With Me" comes to mind as it's pretty much her and Liam's story. For real. He's literally dating a cheerleader while she's on the bleachers.

"One of yours." Liam begins to rock back and forth.

"Oh, I don't have my music with me." She hopes Liam can't see through her excuse, but she decides to quickly change the subject. "You know, I can hear the music you blast in your room."

This gets Liam to stop. "You can?"

"Yeah, and it's not bad. And I love that you're a secret Swiftie."

"I don't think it's much of a secret, plus, she means so much to you." He glances at Teffy and she stops swinging for a moment. "And Jae."

His little sister. Because when he looks at Teffy, that's all he sees. *If only . . .*

"But I like how you have something that's just for you," Liam continues, unaware of the dagger that's been plunged into Teffy's heart.

"Everybody's been making a big deal out of getting on the varsity team, but it's also, like, I want to have other things in my life. I have other things I'm into."

Teffy nods along, trying to remind herself that having these memories with Liam does make her special, just not in the way that she wants.

"Like dinosaurs," Teffy says—remembering Liam's dino phase all through middle school. He still has a DINOSAURS AROUND THE WORLD poster in his room.

"Um, yeah, because they're awesome." That flush creeps onto his cheeks.

"And bad horror movies."

"The cheesier the better."

"Remember when we tried to make one?" Teffy's heart warms at the memory.

"Your mom was so mad we used all her red food coloring."

"I think *your* mom was more concerned that we made your bathtub look like a murder scene."

Liam's laughter fills the empty park. "That took forever to clean. I swear I can still see little red blotches every once in a while."

"Is it wrong that I'm craving a red velvet cupcake now?"

"So wrong, but also so right. In fact!" Liam stands up. "Why don't we walk downtown to Amelia's and get some cupcakes?"

"And then watch a horror movie," Teffy adds. It seems that her Saturday has turned around.

"You just described the perfect evening." Liam starts walking. "This is why I like hanging with you, Tefs. I can just be myself."

Same, Teffy wants to add. Things with Liam are so natural. Of course, it's easy because they're friends. Really, really good friends, but friends, nonetheless. Liam and Teffy share a bond of knowing each other practically their whole lives. Why can't it evolve into more? Teffy's parents met in college, where they lived on the same floor—they were friends first before they started dating. There's a reason the "best friends" trope is so popular in romance novels. It just makes sense.

If only . . .

"I can also be your source for a sugar rush," she jokes as they turn off the park onto the road that leads to Main Street. "Oh." Teffy realizes they'll walk by her parents' store if they turn here. "Maybe we should . . ."

Realization hits Liam. "Oh yeah, right, let's go this way instead." They go around the buildings, walking through the parking lot instead. Neither one of them want to talk about the bad blood between their parents.

"Liam!" a voice calls out. A girl's voice.

Teffy spies a group of sophomores hanging out behind Ritter's, including Cat.

This possible romance just turned into a horror story.

Cat comes running over, her hair extra bouncy, and she throws her arms around Liam, then plants a kiss on his lips. Teffy quickly looks down at the ground. She glances at her worn gray sheepskin boots she threw on before she left. She's wearing a bulky cardigan and black leggings, her blonde hair in her usual French braid. And she's not wearing any makeup, while Cat looks her usually stunning self: high ponytail with ringlets, a light blue maxi dress with a creamy suede jacket.

Teffy really is a child. She's so foolish to think that Liam could ever look at her differently, when Cat looks like *that*.

"Hi, Tefs!" Cat says as she's got her arms wrapped around Liam. Only Liam calls her Tefs, but Teffy doesn't know the polite way to tell Cat that. "Liam, I thought you said you weren't up for going out tonight."

"Yeah." Liam shifts uncomfortably on his feet. "The thing is . . ."

As Cat looks at Teffy, her eyes get wide. "Oh my goodness, of course! You could've just said you had to babysit."

Babysit? Teffy is fourteen, not four.

"I'm not—" Liam takes a deep breath. "Listen, I ran into Tefs and we were just . . ."

We were just what? Teffy wants him to finish his thought. It was Liam who asked her to meet in the park, but now she feels like a third wheel.

Teffy's phone pings—it's just her parents telling her to help herself to leftovers for dinner since they'll be late, but she's going to use it as her excuse to get as far away from Liam and Cat as possible.

"Oh, it's the Taylors," Teffy lies. "I'm off to meet my friends. See you later."

Teffy doesn't wait for a response from Liam. She turns her back and begins to walk fast, her chin betraying her by twitching. She feels like her heart is being cut open.

"Bye, Tefs!" Cat calls out to her. "Oh, Liam, she is such a sweet kid. You're so nice for hanging with her." Teffy isn't sure if she was meant to hear the last part, but with Cat's cheerleading voice, it echoed throughout the entire parking lot.

Teffy can't get home soon enough. The second she gets to her bedroom, she's going to pull her curtain tight and stop reading into things that aren't there.

Our Chat (The Taylors Version)

TEFFY📚: I know everybody is busy, but just thinking about how incredibly inspiring it is that Taylor rerecorded her early albums to stick it to the men who betrayed her.

TAY🎉: Is our Teffy entering her vengeful era? All I know is I'd never want to cross you

TS⚽: GIVE ME A NAME

TEFFY📚: Oh, no, it's nothing.

TS⚽: NOBODY MESSES WITH A TAYLOR

TWELVE
mad woman

As Taylor sits next to a firepit with Hunter beside her, she almost can't believe this day has been real or that she wanted to leave when they first arrived. She does belong here. She's been accepted by Hunter's friends, who are funny and included her when they took a pontoon out on the lake, even letting her steer. And Hunter, well . . . he's a dream come true: kind, attentive, and, let's not forget, super gorgeous.

Hunter draws her in even tighter to his side. "You good?"

"Yeah." She's perfect. But as she wraps her arms around herself, she realizes she should've brought a jacket after all.

"Those goose bumps because of me?" Hunter asks before he takes a sip from a Gatorade bottle.

"Can I have some?" Taylor asks, not wanting to get up from the coziness of the fire.

"Naw, you don't want this." Hunter screws the top of the bottle on and puts the bottle in his jacket pocket. "So, what do we got going on this week?"

There it is again. The *we*. Her sister always complained how the guys she was interested in never wanted to commit. But here

Hunter is, already incorporating Taylor into his life. *Their* life.

"Not much." Honestly, all Taylor wants to do is spend more time with him. "I've got to start working on my campaign for freshman class president."

"Class president?" Hunter looks confused. "I didn't know you were going to run for that."

He didn't? How could Taylor not tell him? Maybe it's because she only wants to hear about what's going on in his life.

"Yeah, I have so many things I want to do to make life better at school, especially in terms of representation—"

Hunter pulls his arm away. "Oh wow, that's great. It seems like a lot of work."

"Well, I'm not afraid of hard work, plus, it'll—"

"Yeah, I hope you'll still have time for me." Hunter looks down at the ground.

"Of course!" Although, Taylor is realizing how much work it will be. She still needs to fill out the paperwork, come up with a platform, make signs, get ready for the debate . . . And competing with Hannah will be difficult, not because people like Hannah but because she has money. Hannah already has posters up that were professionally printed. Hannah was talking loudly about bringing in cupcakes with HANNAH FOR PREZ on them for the entire school. *The entire school.*

But Taylor didn't let Hannah get the best of her in fifth grade during the Eras Tour drama, or in sixth grade when she gave out special sweatshirts for the class trip to the Children's Museum of

Indianapolis to everybody but the Taylors (and didn't even have them made at Harrison by Design, which was what annoyed Teffy the most), or in seventh grade when she had her birthday party at Freedom Springs Aquatics Park and invited everybody but . . . yep, the Taylors, or in eighth grade . . . honestly, Taylor could go on and on.

But Taylor is going to be the bigger person. However, that doesn't mean she won't enjoy beating Hannah.

"There's this girl in my class," Taylor starts to tell Hunter, but she's blinded by headlights as another car pulls up. It's been like this all day. With every new arrival, the crowd has gotten a bit rowdier. Everybody else is now gathered near the water, and she's worried Hunter will want to join the party.

Taylor squirms when she sees it's a car filled with senior girls, all put together, while Taylor's hair is still damp from swimming in the lake. She's not sure any of her makeup is still on.

"Hunter!" One of the girls spots Hunter and she comes over to them, teetering in high heels and sporting a very short skirt. She practically sits on Hunter's lap. She shoots a look over at Taylor. "Who's the new kid? Emphasis on *kid*."

Hunter pulls the girl off him. "Serena, behave," he says with a playful wink, while Serena swats at him. "This is Taylor."

Serena ignores Taylor as she stands back up. "What's the fun in behaving?" She lets out a loud laugh. Just like when she first arrived, Taylor suddenly feels out of place. And young. "Come on, I have something to show you."

Serena grabs Hunter by the hand. Taylor silently urges Hunter to stay. She likes it best when it's just the two of them. When she doesn't have to share him or have his attention elsewhere.

"Hunter . . ." Serena starts dragging Hunter by the hand.

He finally gets up. "Okay." Hunter looks down at Taylor. "I'll be right back." He gives her a wink as Serena hugs him from the side.

Taylor's left by herself to study the flicker of the fire. She knows she shouldn't be jealous. Serena's just a friend. But she suddenly feels alone and cold.

Taylor goes to check her phone, realizing she hasn't texted the Taylors in a while, but she doesn't have a signal—it's been in and out all day. She also didn't notice it's getting late. Her parents told her to be home by ten and it's after nine. Taylor starts doing the math and she knows they're going to need to leave soon. She'll tell Hunter when he comes back. Which she's sure will be any minute now.

She looks up to see Serena and Hunter sitting on the end of the pier, her arms around him. Hunter's attention is fully on Serena.

"Hey." A girl with short brown hair and glasses sits down next to Taylor. "You're Hunter's . . . friend, Taylor, right?"

"Yeah, hi!" Taylor gives her a smile but keeps her voice down. When Hunter first brought her over to his lunch table, he told her she was a little loud, so she tries to hold back to make a good first impression.

"Hey, I'm Amina." She sits down. "You okay?"

"Yeah, why wouldn't I be?" Taylor says a bit too defensively.

However, if she's being honest, she's anything but fine right now. Hunter has left her alone at a party, and she can't be late.

"Just saw you by yourself." Amina tilts her head. "How old are you?"

What's with people being obsessed with her age? Taylor's in high school. Besides, three years isn't that big an age difference. In fact, her parents are five years apart. "I'm a freshman," Taylor replies, since why does it matter that she's fourteen? Age is just a number.

"Okay, well, just know you don't have to do anything you don't want to do."

Taylor rolls her eyes. It's like her parents all over again. People need to relax. All she and Hunter have done is kiss. Kissing that she *likes*.

"I'm fine," Taylor snaps. She has four older siblings and parents to fret over her. She doesn't need this random stranger.

"Well, I'm leaving in a few. Do you want a ride home?" Amina gives her a smile that makes Taylor think she feels sorry for her.

Maybe she's just jealous because Taylor is with Hunter.

"I'm good. Hunter is driving me home."

Amina plays with a tassel dangling from her key chain. "You do realize it's not just Gatorade he's drinking, right?"

"Of course I do!" Taylor says, even though she has no idea what he's been drinking. Is that why he wouldn't share his drink with her?

Taylor hears a scream and looks up to see a big splash in the lake. Hunter's and Serena's heads bob up.

"Hunter!" Serena screams.

Hunter lets out a laugh as he gets out of the water. He's drenched.

"Um, I'll be right back," Taylor replies. Taylor knows how much Hunter loves his car and she can't imagine he'll want to drive in it soaked. Does he have a change of clothes? Will he be able to leave in the next—she checks her phone—ten minutes?

Taylor walks down to the pier and feels all eyes on her. The group has doubled since this afternoon. The friends who seemed nice enough during the day when they were on a boat and getting sun on the beach are now fanned out, mingling among the new arrivals. They don't seem as friendly. There are whispers and snickers. The energy has changed.

Curfew or not, Taylor just wants to go home.

"Hey, Hunter," Taylor starts as Hunter is busy laughing at how drenched he is.

"My phone!" he cries out as he pulls his—most likely ruined—phone from his pocket. Then he lets out a string of swears, which causes Taylor's eyes to go wide.

"Not in front of the children!" one of the guys says as he goes to cover Taylor's ears.

Taylor swats his hands away. There are some benefits of being the youngest, and dealing with people older than you who think they're so clever is one of them.

"Hunter," Taylor says in a stern voice.

An "ooh" chorus comes from the group congregating near the pier.

"I need to go home soon," she says.

Hunter takes off his soaked shirt and begins to wring it out. "Aw, come on, babe. We can't leave now. Party is just getting started."

"But my—" She stops herself from mentioning her dad, although presumably all Hunter's friends live with adults of some kind. "I need to get home."

Hunter's face becomes pinched, annoyed.

"Sorry," Taylor says softly. Although, Hunter knew she had a curfew and has repeatedly *promised* her dad she would never be "a second late." And if she is, there's no way her parents will allow her to see him again.

Hunter walks away and Taylor follows him, hoping this means he's going to take her home. But by his clenched fists and the stomping of his wet shoes, she thinks he's mad. At her.

"Hunter, I didn't mean—"

He turns around. "What? You didn't mean to embarrass me in front of my friends?"

"I—" Taylor is confused by how quickly his mood changed. And why is this suddenly her fault? *Hunter* is the one who fell into the lake, or pushed Serena, or whatever. How is Taylor reminding him that she needs to go home embarrassing him? "I have a curfew."

"You're such a child," he says as he walks to his car. "What a shame, because nobody likes a childish bi—"

"Hunter." She stops him before he says something he'll regret. She knows he's not thinking straight.

Then maybe he shouldn't be driving, a voice pops into her head. A voice she shouldn't dismiss. She also can't ignore how unsteady he is on his feet.

Hunter spins around. "How exactly did you think I was going to handle you dragging me away from my friends—"

"I'm not—" She tries to defend herself, but he's talking over her.

"And you have the audacity to be angry with me?"

"I'm not angry." Although him behaving like this is making Taylor upset. She has every right to be annoyed. Hunter has broken a promise to her. To her dad. He's made a fool out of *her* in front of his friends. "I just need to go home."

"Then let's go!" Hunter storms over to his car and yanks the front door open. "Get in!"

There's a lot that's confusing Taylor right now, but the one thing she knows is that she is *not* getting into that car.

"It's fine," Taylor says lightly, trying to change the tone. "I'll get a ride from someone else." She locks eyes with Amina, who holds up her keys. Taylor gives her a nod.

"Taylor, I said I'd give you a ride." Hunter starts patting his jeans pocket for his keys. "So, I'm giving you a ride."

"You . . ." The words get caught in her throat. She doesn't want Hunter to think she's judging him, but she also knows she needs to be smart. He shouldn't be driving.

"Look, I'm so sorry. You stay here. Have fun with your friends. Just . . . maybe have someone else drive your car? Someone who . . .

isn't . . . wet. And I'll talk to you tomorrow. Okay?" She goes up on her tiptoes to kiss Hunter, but he steps back.

"Whatever." Hunter walks toward his friends, who cheer at his return. He doesn't even bother looking back at Taylor.

"You good?" Amina asks her.

Taylor can't speak. Her throat is so tight, she feels like she's being strangled. Taylor stays silent as she gets in Amina's car.

"Listen, Taylor," Amina begins. Taylor is not in the mood for another lecture. "First, Maya and David are drinking water and are in charge of driving people home if things get out of control, which they clearly are. So Hunter will get home safe. But most importantly, never apologize for doing the right thing and standing up for yourself. Especially to guys like Hunter."

Taylor nods, even though she knows she did something wrong. Hunter wouldn't be so mad at her if she didn't.

Our Chat (The Taylors Version)

TAY🎉: Once upon a time—fifteen years ago to be exact—OUR TS WAS BORN!!!

TEFFY📚: Happy birthday, TS! I can't wait to celebrate today!

TAY🎉: And eat so much food. My dad went ALL OUT. We are going to make SUCH A FUSS OVER YOU, TS

TAYLOR🐝: I assume that means lots of cake, I need cake

TEFFY📚: You okay?

TAYLOR🐝: Yes, of course! Happy birthday, TS!! XOXO forever and always

TS⚽: Thanks! Can't wait to see everybody later

TS⚽: I know this is last minute and everything . . . would it be cool if I invited Gemma

TEFFY📚: Yes!

TAY🎉: OF COURSE!!! I wish I had her cool accent

TAYLOR🐝: I may be a little late, have a quick errand to run first. AKA need to grovel to Hunter, I messed things up 😨

TEFFY📚: Oh no! What happened?

TEFFY📚: Although aren't you the one who tells me I apologize too much?

TAY🎉: We have SO much to talk about. OBVS

THIRTEEN
Mastermind

"Happy birthday!" Tay opens the door to TS. She does a little dance as she sings, "You're feeling fifteen and everything will be alright because you get to wear the hat!"

"Happy birthday!" Teffy waves from behind Tay and holds out the hat, which TS proudly puts on.

"Oh, you look nice!" Tay says as she gives her friend a hug. "No athletic tee! Is this a new, more mature TS?"

"Never!" TS sticks her tongue out.

But yes, TS did decide to wear a dark green, flowing sleeveless top with black-and-white-striped shorts over her swimsuit. She just felt like putting a little more effort into today. She also knows how green complements her pale complexion and red hair. Or so she's been told by people who care about stuff like that.

"Happy birthday, TS!" Tay's dad greets her, wearing a birthday hat. "Everything is ready outside."

"Thanks, Mr. Johnson!" TS gives Tay's dad a hug.

"Including presents!" Tay jumps up and down like it's her birthday.

"Well, if there are presents!" TS sprints outside to the Johnsons' backyard. TS will never get tired of spending time out here. There's a huge pool with a diving board and even an outdoor kitchen. There's a big spread of food and presents on the counter.

TS puts her bag down on one of the lounge chairs with an umbrella; she needs to be careful of the sun. She gets more and more freckles every year, which she doesn't mind—it's the sunburns that match her hair that she worries about.

And, of course, no party—or any Taylors-related occasion—would be complete without Taylor Swift playing over the outside speakers.

"My dad made a special mix for you," Tay says proudly. "He asked about your favorite hype tracks, which is way better than what he'll be playing tomorrow, which I assume will just be 'Look What You Made Me Do' on repeat."

"What's tomorrow?" Teffy curls her legs underneath her as she sips pink lemonade.

"Reece is coming over after school to study . . . but I also wanted him to meet my dad." Tay blushes slightly.

"So what's going on with you two?" TS asks. Tay talks nonstop about Reece, but they haven't gone on a date. At least that TS knows of, but she's pretty certain Tay wouldn't keep that quiet. It's not in Tay's nature to keep anything to herself.

Tay lets out a huff of air. "I don't know. Nothing, I guess. I mean, he invited me to watch his band rehearsal last night, which was fun, and I sort of hoped he'd ask me to sing since our voices go so well together, when we did—" Tay stops suddenly and looks over at Teffy. "Um, he took me to an open mic night at the Coffee Cave last week and we sang 'exile' together."

"Good song," Teffy replies but won't meet Tay's eyes.

"Well, if you ever want to do it sometime—"

"No!" Teffy says with a little too much force. "But I can't wait to share those songs I've been telling you about, do you think—"

The doorbell rings and TS jumps up. Taylor always lets herself in, so she knows it must be Gemma. "I'll get it!" She doesn't even wait for a reply and runs into the house. "Got it, Mr. Johnson!" she calls after Tay's dad.

TS takes a deep breath as she opens the door to find Gemma on the other side, her hair changed to light pink.

"Happy—" Gemma's eyes go wide and she looks at TS's head. "Blimey, is that the hat!"

"It is!" TS twirls around. "Iconic, right?"

Gemma's mouth is practically on the floor. "I'm in the presence of greatness."

"*And* the hat," TS fires back at her, feeling a bit braver wearing it. Gemma keeps gaping. "It's one of our birthday traditions. We also watch the video of when we got it."

"Are you going to judge that I watched it on repeat after our pizza date?" Wait. Did Gemma say date? Did she mean it like *date* date? "Because I'm obsessed!"

Gemma isn't the only person obsessed.

"Come on in." TS takes Gemma by the hand and feels sparks flying all around her. "I like your pink hair."

"Huh?" Gemma blinks for a moment. "Oh yeah, I thought you would." She ruffles it and TS is once again mesmerized by the clean, floral smell. "I can't believe we spent most of yesterday together and you didn't mention your birthday."

"I don't make a big deal out of it since it's the start of the season and I can't have any distractions." TS figures she can celebrate her birthday when she's old, like, thirty. But when she got home last night, all she could think about was having Gemma be part of today. TS knows the importance of having a strategy to win a game, and Gemma meeting the Taylors could lay the groundwork for something more.

Gemma tilts her head. "How many times do I need to tell you that you're allowed to have fun, Shaw? Football *is* fun."

"Yeah," TS replies, even though she doesn't remember the last time she allowed herself to really have fun on the field. She's usually busy mapping out her opponents' next moves and focusing on moving quickly and efficiently.

When did it stop being fun? When did it become all about numbers and stats?

Maybe it's because it's all TS wants to do, so she needs to treat it like a job, not a frivolous hobby.

"I think your game would improve more if you weren't always so wound up," Gemma says as she takes in Tay's house.

"Wound up," TS repeats with a frown.

Gemma rolls her eyes. "I just mean that I think if you looked at football more as something you *want* to do than *have* to do, you'd enjoy it more. And probably play better."

TS doubts that. How would doing less make her better? How would laughing instead of intensely focusing get her more goals? How could treating it lightly get her on the US Women's National Team?

"Sure," TS says, so unconvincingly that Gemma laughs. But seeing the brightness on Gemma's face erases her criticism—is it criticism or Gemma trying to be helpful?

"Where are the Taylors?" Gemma asks.

"Taylors?" Oh right. The party. For her. Which *is* fun. See, TS can have fun! TS snaps out of her overanalyzing. "Outside, and you should just know that Tay and Taylor talk a lot, but they mean well, and Tay is probably the most enthusiastic person you'll ever meet, and—"

"Shaw," Gemma says with a laugh. "Relax. If they can put up with you, they must be cool."

"Fair point." She gestures for Gemma to follow her out to the backyard.

"Wicked," Gemma exclaims as she takes in the pool.

"Hi!" Tay comes rushing over and launches herself onto Gemma. "Welcome, and oh my goodness, I've been wanting to talk to you and find out everything about living in London, which has to be so cool, and TS said you saw Taylor at Wembley, which had to be amazing, and I can't wait to hear what your surprise songs were and what you wore and your favorite album and—"

"Told you," TS says with a shake of her head, but she likes that her friends are interested in Gemma.

"Sorry, TS," Tay says as she sits down on one of the lounge chairs. "Gemma, this is Teffy."

Teffy gives Gemma a warm smile. "Hi, we're in Spanish together."

"Sí, es verdad," Gemma replies as she starts taking items out of a Chelsea FC Women's Academy canvas bag: cookies, potato chips, and a present, which she hands to TS.

"Oh, you didn't need to bring anything," TS says, even though she's touched Gemma would with basically zero notice.

"I'm not going to say no to cookies." Tay helps herself to a chocolate chip one.

"And some crisps." Gemma points at the potato chips. "If I've learned anything from moving schools over the years, it's to come with treats."

"How many schools have you been in?" Teffy asks as she takes a handful of chips.

"Four. My mum gets transferred a lot, which makes it hard, but I really like it here."

Is TS imagining it, or did Gemma sneak a glance at her when she said that? She's hoping she did. Hmm, now TS knows what to wish for when she blows out her candles.

"Are classes different here compared to England?" Teffy asks another question, and TS likes how comfortable Teffy is with Gemma.

"Yeah, and it gets frustrating. I've already done the coursework for science, but your history is different. It's a lot shorter than ours in England. You lot are such newbies. My grandmother's house in the country is seventh generation and dates back to the sixteenth century."

"Oh wow. Do you have pictures?" This time it's Tay who is asking. She's leaning forward, interested in Gemma.

TS watches as Gemma fits in so easily with her friends. She has such a soft spot for Teffy and Tay right in this moment. Gemma is in the middle of showing them her grandmother's huge castle-like home when Taylor finally arrives.

"Hi! Hi!" Taylor calls out as she comes into the backyard. Her hair is a bit messy, and she's in a frenzy. "Happy birthday, TS, and sorry I'm late, but, like, the last twenty-four hours have been *a lot* and you're never going to believe what happened. Okay, first—"

"Ah, Taylor, this is Gemma," TS interrupts. While TS doesn't need her birthday to be all about her, she's a little annoyed Taylor has stormed in on a cloud of chaos.

"Hi, Gemma!" Taylor says before launching back into her story. "So, I went over to Hunter's and he was so cute because he had just gotten up, even though it's, like, two in the afternoon, and his hair was all over the place and his eyes were so sleepy. I totally apologized—"

"What exactly happened?" TS presses. It's one of those things that she's not sure if Taylor is being overly dramatic or if it's something that she shouldn't be apologizing for. There's something about Hunter that doesn't sit right with TS. She's tried to bring it up a few times with Taylor, but she's so quick to shut down anything that doesn't fit into the perfect narrative she's written about Hunter.

"Oh, it's silly, really." Taylor shifts uncomfortably on her feet. "We were hanging with his friends and it was getting late. Right before I needed to go home because of my curfew, Hunter fell into the lake and it was hilarious." Taylor lets out a forced laugh. "And he obviously couldn't drive me home so a friend of his did."

"And how is any of that your fault that you needed to apologize?" Teffy asks, her brows furrowed. "He promised to get you home."

"Oh, it's not like that, and Hunter was going to drive me, but he . . . was drenched and I just got upset because I was worried about being late." Taylor lets out an annoyed breath.

"Again, why do *you* need to apologize for that?" TS presses. Hunter basically forced Taylor to get a ride home from a stranger. "Taylor, I don't think Hunter—"

"Like I said," Taylor says with a grimace, and TS can tell this could quickly escalate into a full Taylor meltdown. "*I* was being so dramatic and silly, and I know this is going to come across as a total shock, but I made a scene— *I know, me?* I'm so quiet and demure. But let me get to the best part! Hunter not only forgave me, he *asked me to the Homecoming dance*! Can you believe it?" Taylor shimmies her shoulders and starts dancing around the pool.

As far as TS is concerned, that doesn't excuse what Hunter has done, but she knows better than to stir the pot.

"Oh wow!" Tay exclaims, and joins Taylor in dancing. "That's so cool."

"What's a Homecoming dance?" Gemma asks.

"It's a big dance and, like, a huge deal," Taylor starts to explain, her usual confidence returning. "It's the main part of Homecoming weekend, when alumni come to watch the football game and it's usually one of the biggest games of the season."

"This year the boys' football team are playing the next district over, and we're big rivals so it's going to be pretty intense," Teffy adds. "Liam was telling me all about it."

"Who's Liam?" Gemma asks with a smile. TS loves that Gemma's also interested in her friends.

"He's just my neighbor," Teffy says with a bit of a grimace. TS has a feeling there's more going on there. She can't tell if it's good or bad.

Gemma nods along. "When is it?"

"The same weekend we play Lincoln," TS answers. "That's *our* big match. They won state last year. If we beat them, we'll most likely be number one in our division."

"That's incredible." Teffy starts typing in her phone. "I'll be there."

"Me too!" Taylor says.

Tay scrunches her face. "Um, I have to check since we might be cheering—"

"For the boys," TS finishes for her.

"I can't help it." To her credit, Tay does look disappointed.

"Oh, no, I get it." TS doesn't want to start things in front of Gemma, especially after Mount Taylor has been contained. But it's frustrating that the girls' team gets overlooked. "The cheer squad can't cheer for girls, sure, fine, whatever. But what's *your* excuse for falling over Reece, yet not making time to sing with Teffy?" TS snaps her mouth shut, she doesn't know why she had to say that. She just gets overprotective of Teffy. It takes a lot for Teffy to share one of her songs and she's annoyed that Tay hasn't made time for her. She knows Teffy won't be the one to say it, so TS will.

"Sing?" Gemma asks. She seems genuinely curious, but it also might be trying to defuse the match TS just lit.

"Teffy writes these amazing songs," TS explains. "Tay used to sing them and . . ."

Tay stands up, her arms folded. "I've been asking Teffy practically every day to start a band with me, and we all know why she won't, so don't make it seem like I'm not being a good friend. And for your information, TS, Teffy and I are trying to find a time to go over her new songs. So there."

"Oh." TS looks to Teffy, who gives her a nod, her cheeks flush.

The backyard is quiet, except for "Karma" playing on the speakers. It's beyond awkward. TS realizes this is sort of her fault for doing this on her birthday.

"Well!" Teffy says loudly to slice through the tension. You know it's bad when Teffy's the first one to speak up. "I want to hear more about Gemma's grandmother and her insanely cool house. It looks like the one from *Downton Abbey*. My mom watches that show on repeat."

"They filmed that close to her!"

"Really?" Teffy leans in and starts chatting away with Gemma, while Tay's gaze remains on the floor, and Taylor's focus for the last few minutes has been on her phone.

TS hopes she didn't push things too far. She knew things would be different in high school, but the last thing she wanted was for the Taylors to start slipping away from one another.

". . . so maybe we should all go together?" Teffy says. "TS?"

TS looks up to see everybody staring at her.

"What? Sorry? Was thinking . . . about this play I want to try," she lies. Although it proves that she *can* think about things other than soccer.

"This one is always strategizing." Gemma nudges TS with her shoulder. "If you fail to plan . . ."

"You plan to fail," TS finishes.

"I was just saying to Gemma that we should all go to the Homecoming dance together," Teffy explains.

And the MVP of the party goes to Teffy! TS is impressed that Teffy just came out and asked Gemma. Can Teffy tell TS likes Gemma? She can totally tell. It's like at the match yesterday. TS wishes Teffy could be more upfront about her own feelings, but she's not going to complain. Best. Birthday. Present. Ever.

“Yeah, totally,” TS says. “Should be *fun*!” She gives Gemma a wink. TS can prove to Gemma—and herself—that she can let loose on and off the field. Although to be honest, TS hadn’t really thought about going to the Homecoming dance, but if Gemma is going to be there . . .

“Great!” Teffy replies. “Gemma? You in?”

TS finds herself holding her breath. Gemma turns to TS with a smile. “Yeah, that’d be brilliant.”

Our Chat (The Taylors Version)

TS⚽: Thanks for the most amazing birthday party 🫶🫶🫶

TAY🎉: OF COURSE!

TAYLOR🐝: Sorry I had to go all Taylor when I got there

TAY🎉: WE LOVE YOU! And glad things are better with Hunter

TAYLOR🐝: They are, but I'm so behind on my homework

TS⚽: And your campaign!

TEFFY📚: That's right! How have we not done posters yet?

TAYLOR🐝: I'm not so sure anymore . . .

TEFFY📚: About posters?

TAYLOR🐝: No

TAYLOR🐝: Running

TAY🎉: WHAT? NOOOOOO! You'd be THE BEST PRESIDENT!!! When you shine, you make everybody shine

TAYLOR🐝: It's just a lot

TAY🎉: I get it, I'm so behind, I need there to be two of me

FOURTEEN
Jump Then Fall

This isn't the first time Tay has wondered how Taylor Swift does it all: albums, tours, videos, social media, all while being amazing and generous to her fans.

While *this* Tay is practically drowning in all she has to do: school, homework, gymnastics, cheer practice, trying to be a good friend . . . She can't wait to hear Teffy's new songs. Tay knows they'll be brilliant. They've been trying to get together—Tay knows how much it means when Teffy shares her songs—it's just been hard to find a time. It's not an excuse, it's a fact.

And then there's Reece. Another amazing songwriter. Okay, he's a bit moodier, but he's so cute. If only he saw Tay the same way.

"Dad," Tay starts after school on Monday. "Please be nice."

"Honey, I'm always nice." Her dad gives her a big smile, which is welcoming, but Tay can't help but notice a bit of playful menace behind it.

"Daddy . . ." Tay shakes her head.

Tay and her dad are super close and she's never had a boy over before, so *of course* he's going to be protective. Still. Tay can't help but be worried because, let's face it, Reece isn't outgoing like her and her dad. And Tay really wants her dad to like Reece, because *Tay* likes Reece. A lot.

"Tay, relax. Didn't I help you make brownies for this boy?" Her dad places a plate of turtle brownies on the table in the living room.

"Okay, but Reece is sort of quiet." Tay just wants to set his expectations. He's so used to the Taylors coming over and being, well, the Taylors. Loud. Goofy. Comfortable.

Her dad laughs and rubs his bald head. "Oh, Tay, are you letting the poor boy even get a word in edgewise?"

Okay, yes, Tay can be loud. But she finds herself holding back when she's around Reece. She likes to give him plenty of space to talk since she wants to know everything about him. It takes every ounce of her being to not just keep talking and talking whenever they're together. Because she gets really excited when she's with him, it's hard to keep it in.

Tay is just an excitable person!

The doorbell rings. "Okay, he's here!"

"Oh, is that what the doorbell is for?" her dad teases.

"Dad!" Tay goes to the door and steadies herself. She doesn't want to come across nervous, as that will make Reece nervous. She closes her eyes for a moment, takes a breath, then pulls her shoulders back. When she opens the door, she finds Reece standing there, anxiously kicking at the ground, his guitar strapped around his back. "Hey, Reece! Come on in!"

As Reece enters the house, Tay studies his face while he takes in their living room. Most people usually comment on how big her house is, but it's nothing compared to Reece's.

"Hello, Reece. I'm Mr. Johnson." Tay's dad approaches Reece with his hand held out. Her dad isn't even subtle as he inspects Reece from head to toe, a frown on his face. Reece is in his standard all-black outfit, his hair covering his eyes, and his gaze on the floor.

Reece shakes her dad's hand limply.

"We made brownies!" Tay shouts into the awkward silence.

"I don't like brownies," Reece replies as he looks down at the floor.

"Oh." But also, *who doesn't like brownies?*

"A guitar, huh? I thought you were here to study," her dad comments as his eyes are glued on Reece.

"We are," Tay replies. She really needs to keep her grades up and she hasn't even had a chance to do any of the reading for English or history. She's hoping she and Reece can do their assignment, hang out before dinner, and then she can finish the rest of her homework.

At least that's the plan.

Her dad raises an eyebrow. "And you need a guitar for biology?"

"Oh, well," Tay starts to explain, but she didn't know Reece was going to bring his guitar. She's sort of excited to see what he wants to play. She loves that he wants to share his music with her. That he asks her for her opinion. "We may take a study break."

Her dad doesn't look like he believes her. "And, Reece, what do your parents do?"

"Finance," Reece answers as he shifts on his feet.

"And do they work in town or Indianapolis?"

"Indy."

While Tay's dad grimaces, all Tay wants to do is give Reece a hug. It's clear he's nervous—there's a tremor in his hands, he keeps fiddling with his leather bracelet, he isn't making eye contact. Reece only seems relaxed when he's playing guitar or when Tay does the talking for him. Which is why they'd make such a great couple. Everybody knows Tay doesn't mind filling the silence, especially when it puts Reece at ease.

"Do you have any siblings?" her dad continues. Brian Johnson is not a man who is easily dissuaded. He makes friends wherever he goes; it's something Tay got from him: being friendly.

"One."

A glance at her father, and Tay can tell this is going as badly as she feared.

"A sister, right?" Tay fills in for Reece. She remembers seeing a family picture when she was at their house. "She's older and at college."

"Oh yeah, where?" her dad's focus is still on Reece.

"Purdue," Tay replies.

"I'm asking Reece," her dad states.

"Dad, you're basically interrogating him!" Tay playfully nudges her dad, but she's also a bit horrified that he has bombarded Reece since the moment he walked into the house. "And we've got homework to do."

Okay, Tay is also a bit frustrated that Reece didn't seem to put much effort into talking to her dad. Maybe it's not as important to him as it is to her. Maybe because he only sees Tay as a friend. A biology partner.

"Come on, Reece." She motions for Reece to follow her down the hallway to her room.

"Keep the door open!" her dad calls out after them as they enter Tay's room.

"Sorry about him," Tay starts, but she knows her dad is just interested in the guy Tay has been spending so much time with. Someone she wants to spend *more* time with. Someone she'd like to go on a date with.

Ugh. Biology isn't the only thing that doesn't make any sense to Tay.

"It's okay." Reece sits down on the floor. "Parents put me on edge. Thanks for filling in."

"Yeah, my dad can be a bit intimidating." Even though Tay knows he's just a big old teddy bear.

"I wouldn't mind if you also did the oral presentation in class."

"Of course! We all know I don't have a problem speaking." Maybe she should also offer to be the front woman of his band? How amazing would that be? She'd be like Hayley Williams of Paramore—the girl in front of the guys.

Reece's shoulders start relaxing. "That's what I like about you, Tay. You don't force me to speak . . . you just let me be."

Tay makes a mental note: Start talking even more around Reece. Like that will be a problem.

"Okay, then let me talk and talk and talk!" Tay sits down next to Reece and pulls out her biology book and assignment worksheet. "Although I unfortunately don't know as much as you about this stuff, but I thought we could start with cell structure as I still get confused between—"

"Wait, you really wanted to study?" Reece leans his back on the wall and curls his legs out. He's so much more relaxed when it's the two of them. Reason 1989 why they should be together!

"Oh, um, yes? I need to keep my grades up."

Reece smiles at her and her stomach does a kick double full twist. "You helped me back there with your dad, so let me help you." Reece takes Tay's worksheet and starts filling it out.

"Oh, ah . . ." Isn't that cheating? She knows they're partners, but the worksheet is supposed to be done by each individual. And she really wants to understand the assignment since they'll be tested on it next week. Although whenever Reece tries to explain a lesson, Tay has trouble staying focused: She gets lost in his pale eyes and she keeps staring at his lips. Besides, all she wants to hear from Reece is that they should be together.

Instead, he finishes her worksheet. "Now you're done."

"Ah, thanks!" She tries to sound grateful, but she wishes he would've asked her before he simply filled it out for her. But it's done, so she'll just focus on the future. *Their* future. "Oh! I got you a special study treat." Tay pulls out a packet of Skittles from her backpack. She noticed Reece had them during his band's practice on Saturday.

"Thanks." He opens the bag, then grimaces. "But I don't like the yellow ones."

"Are there bags without yellow?"

"No, they're usually taken out." Reece doesn't fill Tay in on who is supposed to take them out, maybe the maid? "I read about a rock band that used to demand no brown M&Ms backstage and I sort of think that's cool. I don't like yellow Skittles, so I have them taken out."

"Oh." Tay pours out the Skittles on a plate. Reece just looks down at them. Um, can't he just pick around them? Tay wants to roll her eyes since it's a pretty ridiculous request, since he's not a rock star *yet*, but also, it's really not *that* big of a deal. She takes the yellow ones out. Honestly, Tay didn't really think there was a taste difference between any of the colors. She usually just puts a bunch in her mouth.

"It's one of the things I'm going to put in *my* rider."

"What's a rider?" Tay asks, happy to have the awkwardness with her dad behind them.

"It's a list of things you require backstage before a performance, like no brown M&Ms. There are some artists who make pretty out-there demands. I've read online that, like, Justin Bieber asks for ten luxury sedans and Justin Timberlake needs to have an elevator for himself as well as an entire floor." Tay knows better than to believe everything you read online; however, she is starting to think artists named Justin are trouble. "And then there's Kanye West, who—"

"I'm *not* going to let you finish," Tay interrupts Reece, causing him to laugh. It's not something he does often, but it's one of Tay's favorite sounds. She wishes her dad could see *this* version of Reece.

"Really?" While Tay thinks it's all a bit excessive, she's also glad he didn't mention Taylor Swift. She couldn't imagine Mother forcing people to pick out different-colored Skittles just because she could.

"What would you put in yours?" Reece helps himself to the pile of non-yellow Skittles.

"Oh, well, I really like cupcakes. And, um . . . maybe flowers?" Tay thinks she'd just be happy to perform, without making someone go out of their way to be difficult.

"You need to make sure people treat you the way you're worth," Reece says. Then he leans in. "Because you're worth a lot, Tay."

As he gets closer, Tay finds herself frozen. Oh my goodness! Is this really the moment she's been waiting for! Is Reece going to kiss her? Her heart starts beating faster as Reece is only inches from Tay. Then Reece takes his hand and reaches . . . behind her to grab his guitar.

Seriously! Tay tries to hide her disappointment, but it's hard. She's not that great an actress. So she puts on a huge smile as he starts strumming his guitar, before singing a new song to her. She loves that he's so open with his music. That he wants to share it with *her*. When Reece finishes, he pulls out a notebook. "Okay, now your turn." He points at the lyrics.

Oh wow. WOW. Reece wants Tay to sing one of his songs.

She knows how important his music is to him, and for him to ask Tay to sing his songs, well, that has to mean *something.*

Reece plays through it one more time for Tay to get the melody, and then she sings. She begins, a bit higher than him, *"Don't you worry about my pain, don't you worry when it rains."*

"Okay." Reece stops. "You've got such a nice, clear voice."

Tay finds herself blushing. She's going to tell her dad at dinner how wonderful and complimentary Reece is. How he acts when he's behind a (not really) closed door.

"But you're a bit too cheerful when you sing," Reece continues. Tay can't help it, she *loves* singing. It makes her happy! And singing one of Reece's songs! How could she NOT be beyond thrilled? "And this song is about loss. It's about longing. Try it again, but with more angst in your voice."

Tay really isn't an angsty type of girl. But she realizes singing is also performing. And Reece knows about performing—he's in a band, after all—so she wants to learn from him.

They play the song a few more times, Tay changing her voice, wanting to get Reece's approval.

"Let's go one more time."

"Okay!" Although, honestly, she's sort of sick of the song, but this is what you have to do to be good. Practice, practice, practice, just like she does with new tumbles.

Plus, she likes the way Reece is looking at her. His gaze keeps shifting to Tay's mouth. Maybe he's afraid to take the leap and ask her out. Maybe they could jump in together.

When she finishes, Reece leans in again and Tay knows this is it. Reece is going to kiss her. Tay closes her eyes, wanting to fully take in Reece's lips on hers and—

"So, we're all done with studying, I see," comes Tay's dad's voice.

Tay pulls away quickly. "Um, yeah, we were just singing and . . ."

They've totally been busted. At least, Tay hopes Reece really did want to kiss her, because she wants to be with him so much. SO MUCH.

"I should go," Reece says as he gets up. His shoulders are back up to his ears. That ease he had when he was playing—when it was the two of them—is gone.

"Yes, I think that would be best." Her dad keeps his focus on Reece until he leaves. He didn't even let Tay have a moment alone with him to say goodbye.

"Daddy," Tay begins. She can't believe how cold and downright rude he was to Reece.

"Tay, that boy isn't right for you."

"You don't even know him," she defends Reece. "There's this sweet side you don't see, he just gets anxious around you. And do you blame him?"

"Tay Tay." Her dad is the only one who still calls her that. "I'm not going to apologize for being protective of you."

"We're just class partners!" Tay hates to admit it, but it's true. "Do you want me to fail biology?"

"You know this isn't about biology."

Tay wants to get mad, but she knows how to play her dad. "Daddy, I'm a good kid. Don't you trust me?"

"I trust you. The thing is, I don't trust him."

"You wouldn't like any boy I bring home."

This gets her dad to smile. "Well, that's true."

"Just trust me." Tay then stomps back to her room and makes a big production of shutting her door loudly.

Perhaps Tay has the capacity to be angsty after all.

Our Chat (The Taylors Version)

TAY🎉: GUESS WHAT? Reece just texted to tell me the Archers are performing at THE HOMECOMING DANCE!!!

TAYLOR🐝: WHAT? The countdown has officially begun: 3 weeks to Homecoming!

TAYLOR🐝: Oh! What if he asks you to join him onstage like tomorrow

TEFFY📚: What's tomorrow?

TAY🎉: We're doing the open mic again at the Coffee Cave

TAY🎉: You should come, Teffy!

TAYLOR🐝: I'll be there! WITH HUNTER. SWOON! Come on!

TAY🎉: Yeah, come on, Teffy!

TEFFY📚: Sounds cool.

FIFTEEN
Untouchable

Teffy doesn't want to be a jealous type of person. She likes supporting her friends. But still. It stings that Tay didn't tell her that she was doing an open mic night. Like she's keeping it from Teffy. And, of course, when Teffy is finally ready—and excited—to share her new songs, Tay has been too busy. Tay has time for Reece, but not for her.

All Teffy seems to have is time.

At least there's one thing Teffy has to look forward to every day. Meeting Liam at the park after dinner. It's become a routine. Something between the two of them.

Even if he only sees her as a kid, it's better than not seeing her at all. Teffy just has to remind herself to not let her feelings get carried away.

Which should be easy enough, but then her heart does a traitorous flutter when she sees him waiting for her on Tuesday.

"Hey, Tefs." Liam's face lights up when he sees her. "I brought you a treat."

Liam holds out a bag of Trader Joe's Brookie Caramel Candy Clusters.

"Oh, my favorite!" Teffy takes a piece of the brownie and cookie concoction.

"I know you like salt with your sweets." Liam happily pops a chunk into his mouth.

"Are you calling me salty?" She puts her hand on her hip and juts it out, trying to give attitude.

See, Teffy can never be this casual—although some may call it flirty—with just anyone.

Liam laughs. "Ah, *no*, I just remember that you ate my mom's salted caramel brownies so quickly nobody was able to get close to the pan."

"That's not true." Even though it was.

"Tefs, I've never been one afraid to dive into food, but you get this look where even *I* know it's time to back away." Liam holds up his hands. "But you really have to share these with me because Coach told me to bulk up." Liam flexes his arm, which looks perfect to Teffy. "I know I'm supposed to do it with chicken breasts and eggs and protein powder, but this is way more fun." He puts a huge piece in his mouth, chewing with his usual vigor. A few crumbs come tumbling onto his shirt. There's chocolate on the side of his mouth. On anybody else, it would be a little gross, but Teffy's always found Liam's sloppiness endearing.

"Come to think of it, *I* need to bulk up for winter," Teffy jokes as she takes another handful. "Although I'm sure TS would be happy to swap protein shake recipes with you. She once convinced me to take a sip of this green juice she was drinking by telling me it tasted better than it looked, and guess what, it didn't. I nearly choked." Teffy shudders at the memory.

"I wish I had the focus TS has," Liam admits. "But it's clear she wants it more: to be that elite athlete."

This surprises Teffy since Liam spent so many afternoons in their backyard playing football with his brother and Charlie. Teffy usually kept them company by reading a book. "I thought you wanted to play."

Liam looks out at the pond. "Yeah, I do. It's fun. But I don't want to be someone who eats, drinks, and sleeps football, you know? I want a balanced life, and I just feel all these people are sort of pushing me into a corner." He shrugs before looking at Teffy. "But not you, Tefs. I can always just be myself with you."

Same, Teffy wants to tell him, but she's speechless as Liam's gaze is so focused on her. Whenever they're together, she feels caught in him, she can't think past him. She looks up at the night sky, and tries to find Liam's name spelled out among the stars.

Liam finally looks down at the grass. "Yeah, and I realize I owe you an apology for the other night. My friends can be jerks sometimes and I should've walked you home. I shouldn't have gone out with them. And Cat . . ." Teffy's stomach drops at the mention of Liam's girlfriend. "Well, I think she's jealous of you."

"Cat's jealous of *me*?" She lets out a scoff. Because he has to be joking. Cat is this gorgeous sophomore cheerleader, she's dating Liam . . . Why on earth would Cat be jealous of Teffy?

"Come on, Tefs, you've known me my entire life. We have this bond." Then Liam quietly adds, "And I do talk about you a lot."

Teffy, don't you dare *read too much into that.*

There's a silence between them. Unlike with most people, it's a comfortable silence. Liam doesn't require Teffy to talk when she doesn't want to. Yet she finds herself blurting out, "Have you ever been to the Coffee Cave?"

"The coffee place on Main? Yeah. Once." Liam wrinkles his nose. "It's a bit too dark and pretentious. It's like coffee service with grit and self-importance."

Teffy cringes. Now she really wishes she didn't agree to go. At least Taylor will be there, but she'll be with Hunter. And Hunter isn't . . . He's just . . .

Okay, Teffy can admit it, at least to herself: She doesn't like Hunter. The few times she's been around him, he talks over everyone. And then the other day, when Taylor told them about the lake, all Teffy could think about was that Hunter was in the wrong, and that Taylor falling over herself to apologize *for something that wasn't her fault* was very un-Taylor.

"Why are you asking about Coffee Cave? You want some caffeine to go with our sugar?" He holds up the Brookie bag.

"Tay is performing at an open mic tomorrow night."

Liam's face scrunches up in this adorable way, when he's trying to make sense of things. "Is she doing one of your songs?"

"No, she's been hanging out with Reece Matthews."

Liam lets out a laugh. "The quiet emo guy? He's so not Tay's style."

"Right?" Teffy's noticed Tay has started wearing more muted colors since hanging with Reece. Yesterday she wore a long gray T-shirt with black leggings.

While Teffy thinks people should wear what they want, she has a feeling Tay is only doing it to impress Reece. It's like Taylor with Hunter. Her friends shouldn't have to change themselves to be with someone. Shouldn't these guys like her friends for who they are?

"Are you going tomorrow night?" Liam asks.

"Yeah, I told Tay I would." Even though she regrets it.

"Well, do you want company?" he offers.

"Really?" It would be easier sitting there watching Tay perform with someone else if Liam was with her. Honestly, everything is much better when she's with Liam. Then Cat's words echo in her head. "Do you think I need a babysitter?"

Liam sighs. "Come on, Tefs. I don't see you that way."

Perhaps, but the thing is, she wants Liam to see her as more than his park buddy.

The next night, Liam is standing outside the Coffee Cave. He's texting on his phone, with an annoyed look on his face. When he looks up and spies Teffy, his face changes. It's happy. Brighter than the sun. Those dimples on full display.

"Thanks so much for doing this with me," Teffy tells him. "It means a lot."

Teffy couldn't bear the thought of walking into that place alone to watch Tay performing with Reece and Taylor falling over Hunter.

"Of course, although maybe I should be wearing all black and appear to be tortured and goth." Liam gestures at his royal blue Harrison Eagles hoodie and jeans.

"You didn't get the memo on the dress code?" Teffy spins around in her black peasant top and pants. "Oh, wait! Hold on, I forgot one more thing!" Teffy pushes her blonde hair in front of her face and puts on a bored expression, to which Liam roars with laughter.

Teffy feels so proud of herself, she loves making Liam laugh. Then his face looks serious while he reaches out and brushes Teffy's hair off her face. She blinks for a moment, trying to remember how to breathe.

"W-w-we should go in," Teffy stammers. As she walks down the stairs, she can feel that her face is on fire, probably matching TS's hair. It takes a moment for Teffy's eyes to adjust to the dark din of the coffee place.

"Teffy!" Tay calls out from a table in the front. "And Liam! So glad you came!" She rushes over to give them both hugs.

"Of course!" Teffy says as they approach the table. Reece is slouched over a notebook, writing furiously. "Hey, Reece."

"What's up, man! I'm Liam." Liam greets Reece with his hand up high, at which Reece looks up from his notebook to stare blankly at Liam. "Childhood besties with *this* Taylor." Liam sits down and pulls out a seat for Teffy.

"I feel like I haven't seen you in forever, Liam," Tay says, probably in an attempt to deflect how cold Reece is acting. "How've you been?"

"Good, thanks to Teffy putting up with me and our daily park visits."

"Park visits?" Tay asks, glancing at Teffy. She looks a little hurt that Liam knows something about Teffy that she doesn't, but it's not Teffy who's been too busy to hang out.

"Yeah," Liam continues. "Also known as my favorite part of the day. Well, besides eating and sleeping."

"Hey!" Teffy glares at Liam even though she knows how much he likes to eat and sleep, so she can't complain about coming in third.

"Kidding!" Liam tousles Teffy's hair, like he does with Jae, his little sister.

Sigh.

"Tay, I've never heard you sing a non–Taylor Swift or Teffy Bennett song." Then Liam turns to Reece. "Have you heard Tef's songs? She's an incredible songwriter. I know I'm biased, and yeah, I sometimes have questionable musical tastes, says pretty much everyone, but there's no denying Teffy's talent."

"She is!" Tay says with a little too much enthusiasm. "I've been telling Reece all about it!"

Teffy feels a bit embarrassed from the attention, but it means a lot for both Liam and Tay to say that about her songs.

Reece replies by looking at Tay, like he can't speak for himself. So Tay does it for him: "As we all know, I can't shut up, so, of course, I go on and on about it with Reece!"

"Thanks." Teffy has been really proud of her new songs. "Maybe we can get together this weekend so I can play the new ones for you?"

"Yes, of course!" Tay's excitement has put Teffy at ease, but then Tay's face turns down. "Oh, well, we have cheer on Saturday and then we . . ." Tay's eyes go to Reece.

"Another time!" Teffy says brightly, trying to hide her disappointment.

Reece stands up. Everyone at the table looks at him, expecting him to finally speak. "I'm going to sign us up," he says quietly before heading to the corner with the sign-up sheet.

Liam leans into Teffy to whisper, "He's a ray of sunshine."

Teffy can't help but let out a laugh, and swats Liam playfully. Although she doesn't understand what Tay sees in Reece besides the whole tortured-poet thing.

"Hey, all!" Taylor arrives and pulls over two chairs to their table. "So excited to hear you sing, Tay."

"Yo!" Hunter calls out to the group. "Getting my girl a soda, you want anything?"

"I'm good, man," Liam replies, while Teffy shakes her head before Hunter heads to the counter.

"Are you excited? Nervous?" Taylor asks Tay as she sits down.

"A little bit of both." Tay gestures at the stage. "I know it doesn't look like it, but the lights on the stage are really bright. I can hardly see anything, except the front row, which is why I snagged this table. I want to see my besties."

“Here you go, babe.” Hunter hands Taylor a bottle of Coke. Hunter’s eyes go wide when he spots Liam. “Well, if it isn’t Liam Yoon. Star running back. Good to see you, bro. Excited for the big match?” But before Liam can reply, Hunter continues, “Never been much into ball myself. I tried, was in a junior league when I was tiny. My mom still has this picture of me and I swear I’m drowning in the pads. Can’t believe I was ever that little, you know. It reminds me of the time . . .”

Teffy zones out as Hunter starts telling some story about summer camp. She looks around at the room, filled with older people. They are definitely the youngest—and loudest—group. But Hunter doesn’t notice. He exudes confidence and charm. The table is rapt with attention on his story, especially Taylor. She’s laughing at everything he says.

At one point, Hunter casually puts his arm around Taylor and she leans in so they’re in a sort of half hug. Liam is less than a foot away from Teffy, but it might as well be a mile. How she wants to fit into that crook of his arm. To have him brush her hair away again, but in her dreams he leans in to give her a kiss.

Then a jolt of reality comes in the form of Liam’s phone lighting up with a call from Cat.

Liam silences his phone and puts it away. There’s a part of Teffy that’s excited that Liam has chosen to spend tonight with her. That he didn’t pick up his phone.

But he picked Cat to be with. Liam kisses Cat. Liam most likely dreams about Cat.

Hunter takes a break from his monologue to take a sip of coffee and Liam uses it as an opportunity to get a word in. "So, Taylor, are you going to start prepping for the freshman debate? I've been waiting to see some posters up, you going to do a surprise drop?"

"Oh, I . . . just don't think . . ." Taylor starts, but she looks at Hunter.

"Naw, man." Hunter pulls Taylor's seat so it's right up against his. He puts his hand on her thigh. "Who has the time for pointless student politics?"

"What?" Teffy exclaims. "You're not running? You're going to let Hannah win?"

"Oh, I . . . haven't made my mind up yet," Taylor says in such a small voice, Teffy hardly recognizes it coming from one of her best friends.

"You haven't?" Hunter asks.

"I just, um . . ."

Hunter's phone goes off. "Oh, my crew is down the street. Come on, Taylor, let's go."

"But we're up next," Tay says as she gestures at the stage, where a white guy in long locs has been playing the bongos. "Just five minutes and we'll be done."

"Oh, um . . ." Taylor starts, glancing at Hunter, who stands up.

"I'm sure you'll be great." Hunter gives Tay a wide smile. "But I just don't want to keep my friends waiting, you understand, right?"

"It's *five minutes*." Teffy realizes that loud, annoyed voice came from her. "Taylor, we're here to support Tay, you've got to stay."

Taylor looks at Hunter's outstretched hand. She bites her lip, while Teffy wills Taylor to stand up to Hunter. To stand up for herself. This girl who looks so unsure of herself isn't the Taylor Perez that Teffy knows.

She doesn't know who this is.

"Um . . ." Taylor says as she bites her lip. "We really should go." Taylor takes Hunter's hand and gives the group an apologetic smile before leaving.

Tay looks down at the table, disappointment flooding her face. Liam clenches his fists next to her, while Teffy, for the first time in her life, wants to punch something.

And that something looks like a smug senior's face.

The MC's announcement comes over the speakers, interrupting her thoughts. "Up next we've got an acoustic song from Reece Matthews and Taylor Johnson."

Teffy starts cheering, making up for Taylor's absence. "You're going to be great, Tay!" She hopes Taylor's abrupt departure doesn't affect her performance.

Tay gives her a big smile, but it doesn't reach her eyes. "Thanks, Teffy."

Teffy pushes down the feeling of jealousy as she sees Tay take the stage with someone who isn't her. It's not like she wants to be up onstage, it's just that she feels like she's been replaced. It's Reece who is sitting next to her on an acoustic guitar. It's Reece who Tay has made time for.

Just like it's Hunter who Taylor is choosing over her friends.

Or Liam choosing Cat.

What about Teffy?

Reece starts strumming a few minor chords, complementing Teffy's moody vibe. But then Tay starts singing, and Teffy's mouth nearly drops open at how low Tay's voice is. How it's completely devoid of personality. Tay's face is scrunched up as she sings about loss and heartbreak.

Oddly enough, Teffy's mood improves during the song. The thing is, Teffy isn't an egotistical person. There probably isn't anybody who would accuse her of being full of herself, but Teffy knows one thing for sure: Her songs are so much better.

Teffy practically sprints to the park Thursday night after dinner to see Liam. It's almost as if she waits all day for these moments when it's just the two of them. Plus, she can't wait to break down last night. They couldn't *really* talk with Tay and Reece sitting next to them, and then Tay's dad gave Teffy a ride home.

Teffy arrives at the park to find it empty. Liam is usually waiting for her, but he's not here. Teffy sits on the swings. *Come on, come on . . .* she keeps repeating in her head, impatient to see Liam.

It feels like a million minutes have passed when Liam finally shows up. "Hey, Tefs! Sorry I'm a little late, I was talking with Cat and time just slipped away."

It's as if a cold splash of reality douses Teffy. Because Liam will always choose Cat because she's his girlfriend, while Teffy is just . . . Tefs. While she knows this with her head, it's her heart that can't seem to let go.

"Oh, it's okay," Teffy says, feeling her throat tighten. "I, um, brought you something as a thanks for being stuck in the winter of Reece's discontent."

Liam pushes his hair in front of his eyes and slumps over, in a pretty spot-on imitation of Reece. "Thanks," he says in a moody voice, before returning back to normal Liam. "Seriously, what was that? Why is Tay singing with him? You're a way better songwriter. I smile when I hear your songs. I wanted to, like, walk in a cemetery during a thunderstorm after that."

"Yeah." She looks at the plastic container in her hands and tries to shake this sinking feeling. "Oh well! I made energy bites: They've got protein powder and chia seeds, but also peanut butter and dark chocolate so they taste really good." TS was more than happy to send Teffy some recipes when she mentioned it at lunch.

"Nice!" Liam takes one of the round balls and lets out a groan of delight when he takes a bite. "You know the way to my heart." Liam pats his stomach.

Teffy smiles, but she also knows there's no way to Liam's heart. It belongs to someone else. She knows she's making things worse by looking forward to their time together. Liam was a whole eight minutes late and Teffy nearly came undone.

Liam's face turns serious. "So, listen, I got a weird vibe from Hunter. Dude is just too much, you know? Like, super full of himself and I did not like him bossing Taylor around. *Taylor!* Even *I'm* intimidated by her, but last night . . ."

"Yeah, she was . . ." *More like me*, Teffy thinks. It's not bad to keep to yourself, but that's never been Taylor's style.

Liam grimaces. "I asked around, and whoa, did I get an earful from Cat and a couple of her friends. Hunter always goes for younger girls, he totally love bombs them, bosses them around, until he gets bored and then dumps them."

Oh no. Teffy's stomach bottoms out. While she doesn't like Hunter, she didn't think he could be so cruel. She also knows how much this could devastate Taylor. She likes him so much. She might not run for class president because of him. Sure, Taylor says it's because she's busy, but she's busy with him. Hunter says jump and Taylor doesn't even ask how high, she just does it.

Liam gives Teffy an apologetic frown. "Yeah, just thought you should warn Taylor."

"Oh." And here Teffy didn't think she could feel any worse. Because, *of course*, she should say something to Taylor. She should try to protect her friend, but she also knows that Taylor won't want to listen. That Taylor might not believe Teffy. That, after everything they've been through, she'll believe Hunter over Teffy, because Teffy knows how Taylor feels about Hunter. "Yeah, I'll talk to her."

Teffy feels sick to her stomach. That is not going to be a fun conversation.

"Good, Taylor can do so much better."

Teffy looks at Liam, she wants to say the same thing to him. He's so nice and sweet and it's not like Cat isn't, but she doesn't get him like Teffy does.

"I saw that the new Jordan Peele horror movie is streaming if you want to come over this weekend to watch it," Teffy throws out. "I mean, I'll need to make sure my parents aren't around, but they've been spending so much time at the store, unless I can come around to yours."

"Oh yeah . . ." They haven't really talked much about their parents' feud since it doesn't have anything to do with Teffy and Liam, but she doesn't know if her parents would want Liam over. Or if she'd be allowed in his house. A house she's spent so much of her life in. "I'd love to—and it has nothing to do with whatever's going on with our parents, it's just, I have plans. With Cat. It's our six-month anniversary and I promised I'd get dressed up and, like, comb my hair and be presentable, if you can imagine such a thing."

Of course, he has plans with Cat. His girlfriend. Of six months.

While Teffy has nothing.

There's an awkward charge in the air, which usually doesn't happen when they're together. Liam holds up an energy bite. "Thanks again for these. You're the best, Teffy."

"Stop." As much as she wants to hear that from Liam, she knows they're only words. If Teffy really was "the best," then why is Liam with Cat and not her?

"No, for real, Tefs, you're the best."

"Just stop," Teffy snaps. As she gets up from the swing, a wave of exhaustion sweeps over her. Teffy is just so tired. Tired of being pushed aside. Tired of not speaking up. Tired of Liam not seeing what's in front of him.

"Are you okay?" He reaches out to Teffy, but she steps away.

Teffy feels a sting behind her eyes. She's been fooling herself, thinking she can spend all this time with Liam and that her feelings wouldn't overtake her. That his feelings would change.

Suddenly, the park feels like it's closing in on her. "I need to go."

"Wait, Tefs, talk to me," Liam pleads as he gets up to stand next to her. "Is it what I said about Hunter? I'm only trying to help."

Teffy looks at Liam and can tell he doesn't get it. He doesn't get her. "I need to go," she repeats, and starts walking home. Fast.

There's a part of Teffy that expects—hopes—Liam will chase after her. Will fight for her.

He doesn't, because why would he?

By the time Teffy arrives home, the tears are already falling down her face. She wipes them as she opens the front door and finds her parents sitting at the kitchen table.

"You're home," her mom says with a sad smile. "We need to have a talk, come sit down."

Great, even more bad news. Because Teffy can tell by the upset looks on their faces that her evening is going to get worse.

"What's going on?" Teffy asks, the words feeling like a weight. It's all becoming too much. First, she has to have a difficult talk with

Taylor tomorrow. Second, she knows she can't go back to the park. She can't keep doing this to herself.

"Where have you been?" her dad asks.

"I went for a walk." It's technically not a lie since she has to walk to and from the park.

Her mom frowns. "I didn't think you would lie to us."

"I'm not—" Teffy begins but her dad cuts her off.

"We drove by the park and saw you with that boy."

"That boy?" Teffy repeats. "You mean Liam Yoon." Saying his name causes an ache in her heart. "Son of your best friends."

"Ex-friends," her father says with a scowl. "After everything the Yoons have put this family through, that you would sneak out to see—"

"I wasn't sneaking." Even though Teffy never told her parents why she was going out after dinner every night. With everything going on in her life, she doesn't need this right now. "Are you really going to let business get in the way of our families' friendship? Because I can't—"

"Enough!" her father snaps. "Apparently, I didn't make myself clear, so I'm going to say this only one time: You are not allowed to see Liam Yoon again. Period."

Teffy wants to argue. She wants to make her parents realize how unfair they are being. But she doesn't have it in her. If Liam isn't willing to fight for her, why should she fight for him?

"You know what?" Teffy stands up. "That's fine by me."

Our Chat (The Taylors Version)

TAY🎉: TWO WEEKS UNTIL THE DANCE!

TS⚽: AND MY TEAM'S BIG MATCH!

TAY🎉: THAT, TOO!!

TAYLOR🐝: Need to get a new dress, I am NOT wearing one of my sister's hand-me-downs

TAY🎉: DRESS SHOPPING PARTY!!!!

TS⚽: OK

TAYLOR🐝: Question: who knows TS's password since she's clearly been hacked?

TS⚽: Ha ha

TAY🎉: TAYLOR SHAW, ARE YOU EXCITED ABOUT WEARING A DRESS?

TS⚽: Define the word excited

TS⚽: And when you have this reaction you wonder why I don't share more . . .

TAY🎉: ARE YOU SAYING WE'RE TOO MUCH?

TS⚽: That would be the polite term 😉

TAYLOR🐝: You love it. YOU LOVE US.

TS⚽: 🫶

SIXTEEN
hoax

Despite ignoring the group chat, it seems that Teffy *is* on her phone. Because she just sent Taylor a message asking to meet her before school Monday morning.

TAYLOR🌼: Hunter is taking me to school, can we chat at lunch?

TEFFY📚: How about after school? Will just be a couple minutes.

Poor Teffy. Taylor knows Teffy has never been as loud and in your face as her and Tay, but she's been extra quiet lately. She's mentioned issues with her parents and the store, so she probably just really needs a friend right now, which is exactly what Taylor will be for her.

TAYLOR🌼: Of course, anything for you

And Taylor means it.

Not everybody can find their place in high school as easily as Taylor. She already has a nice rhythm: Hunter picks her up, sometimes he brings her a muffin or donut. She hangs with him at his locker. Then lunch with the Taylors. Hunter usually comes by for a quick kiss before he goes to hang with his friends. Then he takes her to his house or a friend's house.

So, really, there's no time for being class president. Even though it killed Taylor at lunch today when Hannah was passing out her HANNAH FOR PREZ cupcakes all while wearing a MISS PRESIDENT sash. None of the Taylors took a cupcake out of solidarity, even though they don't understand why Taylor doesn't want to run anymore.

Well, it's not that she doesn't *want* to, it's just she can't have it get in the way of living her best life. With Hunter.

"I just need a couple minutes," Taylor tells Hunter Monday after the final bell. "I promised Teffy I would talk to her."

Hunter leans protectively over Taylor's locker. She falls into his chest and he kisses the top of her head. "Didn't you talk to her at lunch?"

"I think she needs to tell me something private."

"Ah." Hunter nods knowingly. "Girl talk."

"Exactly!" She kisses him on the cheek. She loves how much Hunter gets her and understands she sometimes needs to do things for her friends.

"Oh, I got you one of these." Hunter pulls a white box out of his bag.

"For me!" Taylor loves that he got her a little gift . . . until she opens it to find one of Hannah's cupcakes. "Oh."

"Just ignore what it says." Hunter takes his finger and drags it through Hannah's name. "A cupcake is a cupcake, and they're good."

Taylor does love cupcakes—who doesn't?—but seeing Hannah's name gives her a stomachache. "You can have it."

"You sure?" Hunter takes a big bite. "So what should I do while you girls talk?"

"I don't know." Taylor plays with the strap on his backpack. "Pine longingly for me?"

Hunter puts his hand over his heart. "I already do that all day and night."

Taylor can't believe she almost messed this up by overreacting about one silly ride home. Hunter is so perfect, it's unreal.

Taylor sees Teffy approaching down the hallway but stopping when she sees Taylor is with Hunter. "Why don't I meet you at your car? I'll be super quick. I promise."

Hunter looks over at Teffy. "Why do I feel like your friend doesn't like me? What with the look of fear on her face and her relative disinterest in me."

"Who wouldn't love you?" Taylor says, and she means it. Because Taylor thinks she's falling . . . no, she's *in* love with Hunter.

Her heart bursts every time she sees him. She thinks about him nonstop. Like, seriously. It's constant. Taylor wants to spend every waking moment with Hunter.

"You're just saying that," Hunter replies bashfully.

"Hunter, I just . . ." She should tell him. But is this really the time? In the hallway, with Teffy looking like a scared little puppy?

"Talk to your friend, I'll see you in a bit." Then he leans down and gently kisses her on the lips.

Is this real life? Like, seriously?

How did Taylor get so lucky?

Taylor is in a daze as she watches Hunter walk down the hallway.

"Hey." Teffy's voice comes from what seems like a different planet.

Taylor blinks quickly to get back to reality. As head over heels as she is for Hunter, she needs to be a good friend right now. Then she can go back to her supercute and amazing *boyfriend*.

"Teffy!" Taylor gives her a hug. "I'm so sorry I've been so busy and I want you to know that I'm here for you, no matter what's going on. Talk to me." Taylor reaches out and holds on to Teffy's hand.

Teffy's gaze goes to the hallway Hunter walked down. "Um, well, I just heard some things and wanted to tell you as I don't want you to get hurt."

Taylor is so confused, it's almost as if Teffy is speaking a foreign language. "What are you talking about?"

"It's about Hunter."

Taylor drops Teffy's hand. She wasn't expecting this. In fact, she feels like she's being set up. Teffy goes MIA in the group chat, and now she's . . . what? Going to say something horrible about Taylor's boyfriend? Who Teffy hasn't even gotten a chance to know?

"What about Hunter?" Taylor snaps. Why can't her friends—and parents—be happy for her? "Well?" Taylor says impatiently.

Teffy looks down at the ground but then clenches her jaw and looks back up at Taylor. It's a determined look that both impresses and frightens Taylor. She's about to walk away, since there's no way Teffy is going to say anything about Hunter that won't infuriate her.

"I don't have time for this!" Taylor growls.

As Taylor goes to leave, Teffy steps in front of her. "I know you're not going to want to hear this, Taylor, but Hunter treats women, *girls*, poorly. He'll make you think you're his whole world and then get bored and dump—"

"Just stop right there." Taylor is beyond furious. It's that girl from the first day of school all over again. *Of course* people are going to be jealous that Hunter has chosen Taylor. But coming from Teffy, it feels like she's twisting a knife in her back. "Are you seriously walking down Clownelia Street right now? Give me one reason why I should believe whatever gossip—and it's *gossip*, Teffy—is being spread about Hunter. I'm his *girlfriend* and *I know Hunter*. He is *amazing*."

"I just—" Teffy starts, but Taylor doesn't want to hear it.

"I would like to think you'd take my word as his girlfriend over some jealous and bitter girls. And you know what? I'm happy, Teffy. Shouldn't that be all that matters?" Taylor doesn't even let her respond, Teffy should know she's in a winless fight. Doesn't their friendship mean anything to Teffy? Why does she want to burn it all down to the ground by getting in the way of Taylor's relationship with Hunter? "And I just want you to know that when you find someone, I am going to be nothing but supportive. Because you could only be so lucky to find someone as incredible as Hunter, and I really hope you do."

Taylor grabs her bag and storms out of the school, not even giving Teffy a second look. She's close to tears. She can't believe one of her best friends would try to ruin the best thing to ever happen to her.

Hunter is leaning against his car. His face brightens upon seeing Taylor, then darkens when he notices how upset she clearly is.

"Taylor?" he asks with his brows furrowed.

Taylor launches herself into his arms. Those strong arms that feel like home.

"What's going on?"

"I just need a hug. I need you," Taylor admits.

"I've got you. I've got you."

And that's all that matters to Taylor.

To say it's been an awkward few days at the Taylors' lunch table is an understatement. Teffy has been even quieter, which suits Taylor just fine. If you can't say anything nice about someone and all that.

Maybe she should plan something with the Taylors and Hunter so they can see how amazing he is. But *no*, her friends should support her no matter what. Just like she does with TS's sports and Tay's and Teffy's music. Friends support one another. Period.

"You look nice," her mom says to Taylor as she waits for Hunter to pick her up Friday after dinner.

"Thanks." Taylor's wearing a light blue top with baggy sleeves and a tie, with a flared white miniskirt. "I'm feeling very *1989*."

Her mom gives her a smile. "Sit down with your mother."

"But Hunter—" Taylor gestures at the window. She doesn't like to keep him waiting and definitely doesn't want him coming to the door to deal with her parents.

"He can wait." Her mom points at the sofa. "Or would you rather have this conversation with your father?"

Taylor stomps her white Converse-clad feet and plops down on the couch with her arms folded.

Her mother sighs. "All summer you talked about running for class president and I just don't understand why—"

"*I* don't understand why everybody is making such a big deal out of it." Can people just get over it? Obviously, she'd prefer it not be given to Hannah, but she's not going to upend her life solely to beat Hannah. "I've just realized I . . . won't be able to . . . do service to the position."

"Spoken like a true politician," her mom says with a laugh. "I get it, honey, Hunter is cute and—"

"It's not because of Hunter!" Taylor says, even though it is.

"Okay, let's forget about being class president. Let's talk about your grades." *Uh-oh.* Taylor's usually a pretty good student, and, well, she's been distracted lately. Who really cares about equations and history dates when there's Hunter? "I saw that math test in your bag—"

"You're going through my things!" Taylor can't believe her mother would snoop. She gets up, but her mother snaps her fingers, so she sits back down.

Maybe it would be better to have this discussion with her dad.

"Need I remind you that I am your mother, and I will do as I please, especially when my child is hiding her grades from me." The color in her mother's cheeks is rising, which is never a good sign. "If you don't want to run for president, fine, but until your grades get up, no more going out during the school week."

"Mom! I'm fourteen—"

"Exactly, you are *fourteen*. Do I need another reason? Would you prefer I don't let you go out tonight? That I make you stop seeing Hunter? Because if things don't change, that's the next step."

Taylor feels like she's been slapped. Why is everybody against her and Hunter? Taylor's chin starts to tremble. "How could you even think about taking away the one good thing in my life?"

Her mother actually scoffs. Scoffs, like this is some joke! "Oh, really? What about the Taylors? Your family? In fact, I think it's best you stay in—"

Right then a car honks. Hunter's car.

A panic takes over Taylor and her hands start trembling. She can't keep him waiting. "Mom, I can't cancel on Hunter now. I promise I'll get my grades up, in fact they'll be even better. Please," she begs. "I'll share my homework, I'll give you every single thing that I bring home from school. I'll do extra chores. Just please don't do this to me. *Please.*"

Her mom grimaces, and Taylor can feel her heart practically burst out of her chest. Her mom sighs. "I want to see *every* paper, *every*—"

"Thank you! Thank you!" Taylor calls out as she runs out of the house before her mom can change her mind.

"You good?" Hunter asks as she gets into the car.

"Yeah, of course!" Because she's with him now so things are always better.

"Javi texted that the party is already next level."

"Cool." Although Taylor really doesn't want to be at a big, loud party. She wants Hunter all to herself. "Do you think . . ." she starts, but she knows how much Hunter loves being around his friends.

"What's up? Talk to me."

Taylor also knows that unlike her mom, he gets her. He cares about her feelings, her wants, her needs.

"Do you think we could just . . . stay in tonight? Just you and me?"

A bright smile overtakes Hunter's face, which makes Taylor realize she made the best decision to not run. Look at him. Why would she want to do anything but spend time with him? "That sounds like a perfect plan."

No matter what, Taylor is going to make sure she can keep having more of these nights with Hunter.

This, Taylor thinks as she cuddles with Hunter in the basement of his house an hour later. She wishes she could stay like this forever: in his arms. It's like they're the only two people in the world. *This* is worth fighting for.

Taylor starts coming up with a plan: Her parents aren't usually home until six during the week, so she'll just make sure she's home by then. If Hunter wants to do something in the evening, she can use the Taylors as an excuse. Nobody can say no to Tay.

"You're so incredible." Hunter kisses her on the forehead. He looks down at the Hunter bracelet she made him, which he always has on. "Do you think you can make me one with your name? So I can wear it . . . not like I need a reminder of you."

"Of course." She'd do anything for Hunter.

"Thanks." He pulls her in closer. "I'm so glad you asked to do this."

Taylor would always choose this over a party. Over anything, really. "Hunter, you're amazing. I . . ."

"I've never felt like this before, darling." He runs his hand up her side. Taylor squirms when he reaches her waist. He slowly puts his hand under her shirt so his palm is resting on Taylor's bare stomach, which feels like it's on fire.

"Same," Taylor admits. She lifts herself up, so she can look Hunter in those pale hazel eyes. "Hunter . . ."

Taylor is never at a loss for words or even scared to use her voice, but at this moment, she knows that she won't be able to take back what she wants to say to him.

"I love you, Hunter."

The few seconds of silence is almost too much to bear. Taylor studies Hunter's face, which breaks into a big grin.

"Come here." Hunter puts his hand around her neck and draws her in for a kiss. Then Hunter's hands start wandering down Taylor's body and she pulls away.

"What's wrong?" Hunter asks. "I thought you loved me."

"I do, I do . . ."

Here's the thing, Taylor realizes Hunter is more experienced than her. He's older. He's had other girlfriends. This is all so new to Taylor.

Hunter pulls her in closer. "You're my one and only. I just want to be with you, because I love you, Taylor."

He said it. Hunter Brown loves her, Taylor Perez.

"You love me?" Taylor asks. It's almost like she can't believe it.

"Of course." He kisses her again and she melts.

She's in love and is loved. Nothing else matters.

Being in love is as wonderful and amazing as Taylor Swift describes in her songs. Taylor's even in a good enough mood to deal with Teffy at TS's game on Saturday afternoon.

"Go, TS!" Taylor screams loudly from the benches. TS looks up from the side where she's been stretching and gives a wave.

"She's so good," Teffy says. Her eyes keep darting at Taylor.

"She is. And such a supportive and nonjudgmental friend," Taylor adds. Okay, she's going to be a bit petty. It's not as if Teffy doesn't deserve it.

"Is TS . . ." Teffy starts as Taylor watches TS running toward them. "Coming over here? She doesn't leave the sidelines. Ever."

"Hey!" TS's cheeks are flush. "Such a nice day for a game, right? Thanks for coming!"

"Of course! *I* like to support my friends." Taylor digs the knife a little deeper.

"Oi!" Gemma shouts as she comes over and jumps onto TS's back. "You do remember we've got a match, yeah?"

The two laugh as TS runs around with Gemma on her back. She sets her down and TS puts her arms around Gemma. "We're going out later for pizza, you both in?" TS asks over the sound of an impatient whistle. Gemma whispers something in TS's ear and she starts giggling.

Which is very unlike TS, but Taylor likes this side of her. She's definitely been a lot more chill recently. And having fun. Taylor hasn't seen a gross green juice or huge jug of water all week.

"Pizza sounds good!" Teffy replies. "Um, I think the coach is looking for you both."

"Huh?" TS can hardly take her gaze away from Gemma.

Taylor knows that look. It's the look that she gives Hunter all the time.

"You two are so cute together," Taylor blurts out. She wants TS to know that she's happy for her if she and Gemma are more than teammates. It takes everything in her to not turn to Teffy and shout, *See how easy it is to be happy for a friend! Maybe try it for a change!*

"Shaw! Walker!" Coach Callahan blasts her whistle.

"Oops." TS sticks her tongue out. "Anyways, catch you both later, yeah?"

Before Taylor can tell them she's meeting Hunter after the game, TS and Gemma have sprinted back to the match.

“Coach does not look happy,” Teffy says quietly.

Taylor thought her mother was mad the other day, but Coach Callahan is barking at Gemma and TS, waving her hands around. Gemma’s face is serious, nodding along to whatever’s being said, while TS doesn’t look that bothered.

The game finally starts and Teffy stays silent, which suits Taylor just fine. It’s only . . . Teffy has seemed really down lately. Maybe it’s because she feels bad for what she said about Hunter. Because she totally should.

Now, Taylor really isn’t into sports, but she’s seen enough of TS’s matches to know when something’s not right. TS is usually dominating the ball and sprinting ahead of everybody, but she seems . . . distracted. Her focus seems to be elsewhere and she keeps missing the ball. But then again, what does Taylor know about soccer?

Taylor lets her mind wander to her favorite subject: Hunter. She gets to see him after the game, which seems to be going so slowly. While she wants to be here for TS, she also wishes this game would be over already.

“Come on!” Teffy shouts as she stands up along with the rest of the crowd.

“What’s going on?” Taylor looks out and sees TS in the face of the referee.

“I don’t know.” Teffy’s face is scrunched up. “TS let the ball get away from her, which isn’t like her. And now she’s mad.” Teffy shakes her head. “Poor TS. Everybody’s allowed to have an off day.”

"Yes, they are, Teffy."

Teffy sits back down and it's an awkward silence between them as they continue to watch the game. TS misses a pass from Gemma, and when Gemma jogs over to her, TS gives Gemma a cold shoulder. The play is interrupted by the blowing of a whistle.

"Oh no," Teffy says. "TS is being taken out of the game."

"What? Has that ever happened before?"

"No, but I've never seen her act like this." Teffy shakes her head while TS runs off the field and has a heated exchange with the coach, which is also very unlike TS. She goes over to the bench and kicks a water bottle.

"I'm glad we're here for her." Teffy wraps her arms around herself.

If only Teffy felt the same way about Taylor and her relationship with Hunter. Her phone buzzes with a text from Hunter. Where are you?

TAYLOR: At TS's game, remember? It's not going well

HUNTER: Right! Just wish you were here with me

TAYLOR: Me too

Taylor looks at the field. She doesn't really care what's happening now that TS isn't playing, and if she knows TS, she will be in a mood later. What Taylor wants right now is to be with Hunter, especially since her parents think she'll be spending all day with Teffy and TS.

"I've gotta go." Taylor gets up.

"But what about TS?"

"It's TS, she'll be fine, but—" Taylor knows if she mentions Hunter, Teffy will get all weird and she's so not in the mood for it. "I have to go." Taylor sprints out of the game faster than any of the players on the field.

She's got more important things to do than watch a silly game. It's called love.

Our Chat (The Taylors Version)

TAYLOR🦋: ONE WEEK until the dance AND TS's big game!

TAY🎉: Technically 6 days but who's counting

TAY🎉: It's me, I'm counting, it's me

TAYLOR🦋: And I promise to stay the entire game this time, TS

TEFFY📚: Then eat pizza.

TAY🎉: We'll eat SO MUCH PIZZA we won't be able to fit into our dresses!

TEFFY📚: You okay, TS?

TAYLOR🦋: It was just one game

TAY🎉: Just remember to breathe. Relax. It'll be okay

TEFFY📚: TS?

SEVENTEEN
Electric Touch

It's not as if TS doesn't know how to lose. She's lost before—the final match last season where she missed a goal still stings—but she likes to have a winner's mindset. Why do anything if you're not willing to put everything in to be the best?

And not to brag, but TS usually is the best. She's always had that "it" factor when it comes to soccer. She's excelled. She has this natural talent but has worked hard to be better than great. She wants to be exceptional.

But that's not how she's been lately.

TS pulls the blue-and-white-striped duvet cover over her head. It's late on Sunday morning and she's staying in the comfort of her bedroom. Even though she can't bear to look at the trophies that line her bookcase. Or the posters she has of her heroes: Mia Hamm. Megan Rapinoe. Alex Morgan.

She's let them down. She's let her team down. But above all, she's let herself down.

Why? Because she got distracted. She allowed herself to get swept up in Gemma: her laugh, her infectious energy, the spark TS feels whenever they're together. But here's the thing: If you play with fire, you'll eventually get burned.

There's a knock on her door. "Taylor?" Her mom's voice comes from the other side. "You awake?" She opens the door and peeks in.

"Unfortunately." TS keeps replaying yesterday in her head. How she was laughing and goofing around before the game. How she kept messing up, which just made her mess up more.

Her mom takes a few cautious steps, sidestepping the clutter that is TS's room. TS is the kind of person who comes home and throws everything on the floor. But her mom knows this is no time for a lecture, TS has much bigger problems. "Are you okay?"

"No," TS answers truthfully. "All that hard work. And it's like I let my guard down for one moment and . . . poof, gone."

"Everybody is allowed to have a bad day." Her mom brushes the loose strands of TS's hair from her face.

"I'm not everybody." She's Taylor Shaw. She's been Player of the League four times. Now she's not even sure if she'll be playing on Saturday. That's how bad it was. That's how angry Coach Callahan was.

"You put too much pressure on yourself." Her mom lies down and wraps her arms around TS.

"Yeah, well . . ." Maybe if TS was a normal high school player, but she's not. TS wants more than playing in high school and college. This isn't some temporary thing, it's her life goal.

Since she was little, she always answered "professional soccer player" when people asked her what she wants to be when she grows up. It's all she's ever dreamed about. Maybe it's because soccer is what makes her special. It's what people know her for.

"You've been distracted for a couple weeks now," her mom continues. "You're not as strict with your workout routine and diet."

It's true. She hasn't been. She broke her routines and the rules she set for herself, all because of Gemma.

"Well, what do you want? I'm fifteen," she snaps. She's not mad at her mom, she's mad at herself.

Her mom frowns. "Honey, that isn't a criticism. You're the one who said you wanted to be on the US Women's National Team before you turn seventeen, like Lily Yohannes."

"I know, I don't need your pressure." TS moves out of her mother's embrace. She kicks the duvet off and gets up. She starts rummaging through her drawers for her workout gear. She knows the pressure is only coming from her. She's a year away from being sixteen and has so much more she needs to accomplish. She can't believe she let a silly crush get in her way.

It's like she's finally so close to making her dreams come true and then she had to blow it all up. Years and years *and years* of practice and then one bad game—okay, TS needs to be real, a couple weeks of average play from her—and *bam*! Her future is in jeopardy.

"You know we aren't pressuring you," her mom says with a sigh. "Need I remind you, Taylor, that *you* asked to meet with a sports medicine doctor and nutritionist to get the most out of your training, and we did that. *You* wanted to go to soccer camp and we did that. This is *your* dream, honey, if you don't want—"

"Of course I want it! It's all I've ever wanted!" But as TS says it, she realizes that maybe she does want other things. But no, she's worked too hard. She can't give up now. "I'm going to get my head back into the game."

There isn't a lot one can control in life, like how someone feels about you. But TS can be in control of her performance. She can get that part back. On the field. Where she knows she stands.

TS is already strategizing on everything she needs to do this week, the training, the discipline. She knows what will be the hardest part, but it's something she has to do.

"I just want to make sure you're okay." Her mom gives her a hug, and TS allows herself to melt into her.

"I'm going for a run."

"Do whatever you need to do, honey." Her mom gives her a hopeful smile before she leaves.

TS throws on her workout clothes. She's going to run a 10K, that will help clear her mind.

Her phone pings, and she sees it's a text from Gemma: You all right, babes?

TS mutes Gemma on her phone. *No more distractions*, she tells herself before blasting her hype playlist. She runs down the stairs and out the door into the early September air.

She runs. And runs.

Even though TS knows there are some things she can't run away from, she's certainly going to try.

♥♥♥♥

TS is back to her routine during Monday's practice: headphones on, focused, determined. It feels . . . good. Sure, she can have fun—and soccer can be fun—but TS isn't going to waste all her effort and talent when there's so much on the line.

TS keeps her eyes closed but can feel someone sitting on the bench next to her. There's a tap on her shoulder and TS doesn't want to open her eyes because she knows exactly who it is. There's another tap. Unfortunately, it's not so easy to mute people in real life.

TS gathers herself as she opens her eyes to see a worried Gemma next to her. She tries to keep her face neutral, but every time she sees Gemma, she gets this flutter in her stomach.

Gemma mimes removing her earphones and TS begrudgingly does.

"Hey, you okay? You haven't returned my messages. Are you ignoring me?" Gemma looks hurt, and she bites her lip. TS's gaze remains on those lips for far too long.

The thing is, TS isn't okay. But she has to forget about what she *wants* right now. It's what she *needs* to do to get her career—and that's what she wants soccer to be—back on track.

She stands up, determined to make this as quick as possible. "Yeah, I need to focus on practice and getting ready for Saturday."

"Okay, but—"

TS doesn't wait to hear what Gemma has to say. She can't get distracted and that's what Gemma is, one big distraction. TS heads out onto the field and starts running laps. She wants to show Coach that she's back to form. Her teammates start warming up with her, but TS keeps her eyes trained straight ahead.

"You know I can run just as fast as you," Gemma says as she jogs next to TS.

TS stays quiet, focusing on her breath, the feeling of her feet hitting the grass.

"I know Saturday was rough, but it's just one game."

TS picks up her pace, needing space from Gemma and her feelings. TS has always been able to control her emotions. It's something she's conditioned herself to do when she's playing. Never let an opponent see you get frustrated or rattled.

Gemma has done both.

And look what ended up happening.

"TS." Gemma grabs TS by the elbow and TS ignores the spark that travels through her entire body. "TS," Gemma says louder.

TS finally stops in her tracks. "What?"

"What do you mean *what*?" Gemma shakes her head. "What has gotten into you?"

"What's gotten into *me*?" TS points her finger at Gemma. "*You!* That's what. You tell me to relax and have fun, and then I'm an absolute disgrace on the field and *I* get pulled out of the game. I don't know how you play in England, but I've always been reliable. You could bet on me, that's how good I am. And I will not let anything or *anyone* get in my way."

Gemma's mouth is open, her eyes starting to water. "I never meant—"

"Well, you did." TS storms off, running so fast she even laps most of her team.

"Love that you got your hustle back, Shaw!" Coach Callahan says as she blows her whistle to start practice.

"Thanks, Coach!" TS gives her a nod to show her she means business.

Sure, TS's heart may be breaking in two by pushing Gemma aside, but she'll do whatever it takes to bring her soccer prospects back to life.

After all, there's a cost to being great.

Our Chat (The Taylors Version)

TS⚽: Guess who's back to CRUSHING it in practice

TAY🎉: LIKE THERE WAS ANY DOUBT!!!!

TEFFY📚: Yaay! Go, TS! All good?

TS⚽: Yup . . . just a brief interruption in my plan for Soccer World Domination

TAYLOR🐝: And then WE will rule the Homecoming Dance!

TAY🎉: YES! I just need to get through this week and this bio test 😔

EIGHTEEN
Glitch

Tay has always dreamed of being in a band, but being *with* the band isn't that bad. And that's not just her usual try-to-add-a-cherry-on-top-of-everything attitude. It's true!

Tay nods her head along to the Archers at their rehearsal Tuesday night as they practice for their Homecoming dance performance. She likes that she's become part of the group in a way. She's their cheerleader, their hype woman, and they actually like hearing her opinion on their setlist.

And you know what else isn't that bad? Being friends with someone in a band.

Sigh. It's pretty clear that Tay and Reece are supposed to be just friends. And biology partners. And that's fine.

Okay, so yes, Tay still dreams about Reece singing to her and kissing him and brushing his hair out of his face, but she's only human!

"What do you think, Tay?" Reece asks after they finish a particularly depressing song.

She loves that Reece cares about her opinion. That he relies on her to sometimes be his voice.

"Well, you know I love all your original songs," Tay starts, but she also knows that people at the dance will want to, well . . . *dance.* And Reece's songs are more the kind that make you stop and think. She doesn't want to upset Reece, so she chooses her words carefully. "So maybe start with a song they already know, one that's more upbeat to get everyone dancing, *then* you can slow it down with 'Tears from the Heart.'"

Reece nods along and then looks to his bandmates.

"Yeah, man, listen to Tay. She knows what she's talking about," Kai, the drummer, says as he gives Tay a nod. He twirls his drumsticks as he continues, "We should do all covers at the dance and save your moody tunes for the next house party."

"Moody tunes?" Reece's face scrunches up. He runs his fingers through his hair, then Tay notices he's not wearing the bracelet she made for him. Further proof that he doesn't see her *that* way. "I want to share my art."

"Dude, that's what our socials are for," Corey, the bassist, fires back.

"Tay?" Reece looks to her.

Tay knows he wants her to say they should do originals, but she also wants to have *fun* and sing and dance and not . . . well, question all her life choices. The Homecoming dance is not the place.

"Well . . ." Tay gives Reece a warm smile, hoping he'll take the news better. "If you really want your songs to reach a wider audience, you need to leave the crowd wanting more. Then they'll follow your socials and you'll have a bigger online presence. So reel them in with the fun covers and then share your songs in an environment . . . where they can really sit and appreciate the depth of what you do."

Honestly, Tay should consider running for class president with a measured response like that.

Reece nods for a moment before his face turns into the smallest of smiles. "See, you guys, I told you my girl is smart."

Wait a second.

Wait just one second!

His girl? HIS GIRL. *HIS GIRL!*

WHAT DOES THAT EVEN MEAN?

"For the record," Kai pipes up, "I told you to listen to Tay first." Kai gets up from behind his kit and stretches out his dark brown arms.

Tay gives him a smile, but as the band wraps up, her mind is too busy buzzing. So when Reece called Tay *his girl*, did that mean . . . ? No, it couldn't. Could it? He's never asked her out. Study dates, sure. Performing at the Coffee Cave, yeah. He sometimes walks her home from school. But they've never gone on a real date. At least she thinks they haven't. Wouldn't she know? Hunter takes Taylor out to meals. He brings her around to hang out with his friends.

Um, Tay is currently with Reece's friends.

Although they've never kissed.

Or even held hands!

UGH! Why do boys have to be so confusing?

Tay didn't think they had a chance, but now . . .

Okay, enough wondering. Tay needs to get to the bottom of this, and unlike Teffy, she's not afraid to use her voice.

"So . . ." Tay begins after the last band member has left the basement. "Did I hear that right? I'm your girl?" she asks in a teasing manner just in case Reece was joking.

Oh, how she hopes this isn't the one time Reece decides to have a sense of humor.

Reece's cheeks get flushed. "Of course you are."

OF COURSE SHE IS?!?!?

Tay is freaking out inside, but she doesn't want to scare Reece off by breaking out into the most epic cheer routine, because her body is a bundle of excitement and nerves and . . .

SHE'S HIS GIRL!!!

FINALLY!!!

"If you want to make it official." Reece takes off his leather bracelet, the one he always plays with when he's nervous. "For you."

Oh my goodness! Tay knows what a big deal this is.

"Are you sure?" She's so touched he's given it to her, and can't wait to wear it and show it off . . . even though it doesn't fit her vibe.

"Yeah." Reece tenderly takes Tay's hand and puts the bracelet around her wrist. "I don't need it when you're around."

"Thank you!" Tay's beaming as she puts it on. "What happened to the one I gave you?"

"Aw, it was sweet, just a little too . . . kiddie. But I kept it," he adds quickly.

In fairness to Reece, Tay did start making those bracelets when she was a kid.

"And this is also for you." Reece takes a step forward. He places a shaking hand on Tay's jaw, then leans in and gives her the sweetest kiss.

Scratch what Tay thought before: Being in a band would be great and all, but this is truly the stuff dreams are made of.

"I have news!" Tay blurts out before the other Taylors have a chance to sit down at lunch the next day. This news was too big for their group chat. And there aren't enough exclamation points in the world to convey her excitement! "Reece and I are together!"

The three Taylors are oddly silent. "Um, weren't you already together?" TS asks.

"Yeah, I just assumed!" Taylor replies with a laugh. "I mean, you were pretty obvious."

"Well, yeah, but we made it official. Look!" Tay holds out her right hand with Reece's bracelet, like she's showing off an engagement ring.

"Oh, that's so nice! Congrats!" Teffy gives her a smile.

Taylor shoots a dirty look at Teffy. "Yes, of course, we'll support you and whoever you like. I, myself, am over the moon like any friend should be."

While what Taylor said was nice, Tay couldn't help but notice it was done in a very aggressive manner.

But Tay won't let Taylor drama ruin her day. "And I want you to all get to know Reece. He can come across as shy and a bit intense, but he's so sweet. Come over after school so we can hang. Please!"

"I need to run to—" TS begins, but Tay cuts her off.

"Please, TS, please, please, please . . ." She puts her hands together in prayer and bats her eyelashes.

TS sighs in such an over-the-top manner, Tay knows she won her over. "Fine, but I'm running there and back."

"Yes!" Tay claps.

"Of course, I'll be there *to support you*," Taylor repeats while staring at Teffy.

"Same," Teffy says before taking a big bite of her sandwich.

TS looks between Taylor and Teffy. "Well, this should be fun."

Tay's just a teeny bit stressed. Okay, a lot stressed! It's sort of become a constant state between all the demands on her time, but this is different. Tay wants everything to be perfect between the Taylors and Reece. She wants them to get along and for them to like Reece and for him to like them and . . .

Is Tay's eyelid twitching?

"Tay Tay, this might be my best batch yet," her dad says as he finishes his famous caramel brownies with a sprinkle of sea salt.

Part of Tay's plan for this afternoon is to get the Taylors in a good mood with sugar.

"I'm so happy the girls are coming over. It seems like they haven't been here in forever." Her father looks up at her and grimaces.

"We've just been really busy." Which is true. More than true! There's just a lot going on at the moment.

"Yeah, busy with *dating*." Her dad scrunches up his face. "You all are growing up too fast. So fill me in. Anything I need to know?"

Tay pauses for a moment. She used to know every single detail about the Taylors' lives and now . . . "Well, you know Taylor is dating a senior and there's been some tension between her and Teffy. I'm not sure what it is, but Teffy has been really quiet. More so than usual. I don't know."

"You used to know everything about each other."

Further proof that this hang is coming at the perfect time. They have to do a proper catch-up instead of their quick lunches. Then Tay can do her homework and study and practice the routine for Friday's game and . . .

"What else is going on?" her dad asks. "How's TS?"

"She's been extra focused on the game on Saturday; she's back to eating and sleeping soccer. She was spending a lot of time with Gemma, but I haven't seen them together in a couple days."

Her dad raises his eyebrows. "Oh, the London girl who came to her birthday? I thought there was something there. See, your old man can sense these things!" He taps his bald head. "You need to trust my judgment more, because despite what you may think, I do know what I'm talking about."

Tay decides to ignore that slight dig at Reece.

"And your biology exam on Friday?" he presses.

Ugh, bio. Yeah, Tay's eye is definitely twitching. "Daddy, you know Reece and I have been studying."

"Is that what the kids are calling it these days, *studying*?" He rolls his eyes in such a dramatic fashion, he's giving TS a run for her money.

"Daddy." Although if Tay is being honest, she and Reece haven't really been studying. He's been giving her answers, more than explaining. But she'll spend the next couple days cramming and she'll be fine.

She hopes.

The doorbell rings, and for the next few minutes, her house is back to the bustle that happens when the Taylors come over: greetings, hugging her dad, eating food, laughing. Teffy and Taylor sit far apart, but Tay doesn't want to bring it up.

That's what TS is for.

"So, what's going on between you two?" TS points between Taylor and Teffy. "If looks could kill, Taylor."

Taylor puts her nose in the air. "Nothing."

"Teffy?" TS sits next to her and pats her knee for support.

"I just told Taylor some things that I heard about Hunter," Teffy says quietly.

"What kind of things?" Tay asks, curious, but Taylor stands up abruptly.

"*Lies*, that's what! Girls who are jealous that Hunter is with me!" Then Taylor actually stomps her feet, like they're back in middle school.

In what could possibly be the worst timing in the world, the doorbell rings. *No, no, no!* This is not how this is supposed to go! Reece can't walk in on this super uncomfortable atmosphere. He'll definitely want to leave. Or he'll freeze up.

"Can we just . . . chill?" Tay begs the Taylors as she goes to open the door.

Her heart flutters when she sees Reece. At least one thing in her life is going right.

"Hey," Reece says to the floor. Tay takes his arm reassuringly. She knows she'll have to do most of the talking. She just hopes the Taylors won't . . . um, go all Taylors on him.

"Hi, Reece," Taylor says, her voice dripping in honey. "So excited to hang out with you. If *Tay's* happy, then *I'm* happy." She pats the place next to her.

Reece sits down, sinking in the cushions, but his back is rigid. Tense.

"So—" Tay begins, but it's Teffy of all people who cuts her off.

"I *am* happy for you, Taylor," Teffy starts to defend herself. "I was just looking out for you."

"Sure, sure—" Taylor starts.

"Can we not?" Tay says, her voice alarmingly high. She looks to Reece, whose eyes are wide, his shoulders up to his ears.

But, of course, her friends aren't paying attention to how uncomfortable they're making Reece.

"Okay, that's it. Enough!" TS says in her no-nonsense way. "Taylor, if someone told me something that I should know about . . . a teammate or an opponent, I would want to know. Have you ever known Teffy to not have someone's best interests at heart?"

"No," Taylor says quietly.

"And has Teffy ever done anything, *ever*, to purposely upset someone?"

Taylor looks down at the floor. "No."

"And could it be possible that you perhaps overreacted just a little?"

Taylor shifts around for a moment. "Maybe."

"That's what I thought. So! We good?" TS presses.

Taylor nods while Tay takes a deep breath. Reece has rightfully remained quiet, hardly moving a muscle during the exchange.

So much for this going perfectly. It's been a disaster and he's only been in her house for a couple minutes.

"You okay, Teffy?" TS asks.

"Yeah." Teffy gives TS a grateful smile.

"Now that that's out of the way, we can turn the interrogation to Reece!" TS sits down on the floor near Reece.

Tay's dad's laughter comes from the kitchen. "You've always been a favorite, TS."

"Right back at you, Mr. Johnson." TS takes a swig of green juice. Tay can't believe she turned down brownies. "So, Reece, your band is playing at the dance."

"In three days!" Tay replies, excited to get the attention off the Taylor–Teffy drama and back to Reece and the dance. "I've been helping with the setlist."

Reece smiles at her between his long hair, and her heart wants to explode.

"Oh, what songs are you doing?" Teffy asks.

And just like that, the tension in the room vanishes. Tay starts to relax as the Taylors seem to give Reece a chance. Talking about music, the dance. Sure, it's mostly Tay answering for him, but not because Reece isn't interested, he's just shy.

Reece turns to Teffy and opens his mouth, closes it. The room is quiet, everybody waiting to see if he's actually going to talk.

You can do it, Tay wills Reece.

"So, Teffy . . ." Reece starts. "Tay says you also write songs."

"I do," Teffy says way too modestly.

"Can I hear one?"

"Yes! Oh, yes!" Tay volunteers for Teffy. She's getting used to speaking for everyone. It's not that she minds, but it's sort of tiring. "Oh my goodness, Teffy, we can play one of your old ones, but I also know you've been working on new songs, so maybe we can do one of those. If you just play it, then I can figure it out, or whatever you want to do."

Teffy bites her lip.

"I'd really like to hear it," Taylor adds.

It's that olive branch from Taylor that gets Teffy to give the slightest nod.

"Yes!" Tay jumps up and does a kick like she's cheering at a game. Although this time it's a victory for her. Tay's friends are getting along with Reece. Teffy is sharing her new song. Okay, it was a rough start, but it's all turning around!

Teffy digs inside her bag and pulls out a notebook. She hands Tay lyrics to a song entitled "Right in Front of You." Tay scans the lyrics, about a girl watching the guy she loves from afar, how he sees her but not in the way she wants to be seen. There's a line, "*just a glass separating us*," and Tay's head pops up. Is this about *Liam*? How their rooms look into each other's? Is this why Teffy's parents told her she couldn't see him? And why isn't Teffy more upset about it? She honestly seems more angry at Liam. What did he do?

Wow, she really has no idea what's going on with the other Taylors.

Instead of bombarding Teffy with questions, Tay sits down.

"Reece, may I?" Teffy points to his guitar, to which Reece gives her a nod. "Thanks." Teffy tunes it for a few moments before she starts picking a sweet collection of notes. Reece's eyebrows pop up in surprise.

Yeah, Teffy is *that* good.

"Okay, so the verse goes like . . ." She leans in so she can hum the melody to Tay. She does it so quietly, only Tay can hear her.

Here's the thing, Teffy has a really nice voice. It's not as strong as Tay's, but it could be. If she used it more.

After a few run-throughs, Tay thinks she's got it.

"Okay." Teffy starts playing an intro. It's very melodic, something that Tay knows she'll be singing to herself all week. She gives Tay a nod as she starts singing.

The room is quiet, all eyes on Tay. She relishes it, but she also feels much more like herself when she's singing with Teffy and her songs. When she's with the Archers, she feels like she's playing in someone else's backyard, but with Teffy, it feels like home. When she gets to the chorus, Tay looks up from the lyric sheet to see Taylor and TS with their arms around each other, and Reece with his eyes closed, nodding along to the song. Teffy's eyes are down at the guitar strings, even though Tay knows she doesn't need to look to play.

When they finish and the last note of the song rings out, TS and Taylor stand up and cheer like they're back at the Eras Tour. Tay's heart is the fullest it's been in a long time. Her friends. Singing with Teffy. And Reece . . . whose face is oddly blank. He's probably processing Teffy's song like he does with his own.

Tay's dad has come out of the kitchen to clap along. "My favorite band, live and in my living room."

Tay gives Teffy a hug. She can't believe she hasn't made time for Teffy. For this. "Teffy, you're the best! Come over Sunday after the dance so we can perfect it and work on whatever else you're doing!"

Teffy gives Tay a big smile. "I'd love that."

"Isn't Teffy amazing?" Tay says to Reece. Oh! Maybe they could write a song together or something. Include Teffy in his music. It would be the best of both worlds for Tay! Tay goes to hug Reece, but notices he's tensed up. Well, more so than usual. When Tay pulls away, his face has gotten flush, his brows furrowed. "Are you okay? Didn't you like the song?"

"Yeah, it was . . . good. Really good." His fingers go to his wrist, but it's bare.

Tay is about to press, but TS and Taylor start an "Encore! Encore!" chant, then Reece joins them, albeit a bit quieter.

"Tay?" Teffy asks, a smile on her face. "Want to do another?"

Like Tay needs to be asked twice.

Ever since yesterday, Tay has been feeling even better than 22. She's walking with an extra bounce in her step. She's got her music back. She has a boyfriend. *And* she is going to ace her biology test. She even got Reece to agree to meet her at the Coffee Cave after dinner to study, *then* perform.

She can do it all. She can have it all.

Nothing can rain on Tay's parade, except actual rain. It starts to sprinkle as Tay parks her bike downtown. She goes inside the dark basement, which has started to feel like it's her and Reece's place. Where they first sang together. Tay texts Reece that she's there and wants to get a jump on studying so she cracks open her biology book. She's so engrossed in cell structure—who would've thought!—that Tay doesn't realize that Reece is over a half hour late. Which is odd.

But he's busy, too! Tay shoots him off a text and then reads another chapter.

Still no Reece.

Another text. Another chapter, but Tay can't really concentrate. *Where is he?*

Tay goes on social media and notices Reece has recently posted. It's a video of Reece playing with the band, and the caption reads, "REAL musicians jamming."

Um, okay? It was posted ten minutes ago. When he was supposed to be here. He knows how much this exam means to her. How much he means to her?

What is going on? Tay calls Reece and it goes straight to voicemail.

Tay's head starts throbbing. Is he standing her up? And what was that real musician comment? Teffy is as real as it comes. She writes from the heart. Or does he mean Tay?

No, Tay is just stressed about the exam. And Friday's big game. She's making a big deal out of nothing.

Her phone pings. It's Reece—see, she knew she was overreacting to him being a little late. The band probably got into a zone and he'll be here any minute.

Tay reads the text and her stomach bottoms out. Can't make it.

That's it. No explanation. Nothing. What's going on? What has made Reece so cold to her? Everything yesterday was fine. No! It was better than that. It was pure perfection! How could he turn on her so quickly? Tay has been nothing but supportive and patient with Reece. Talking for him. Cheering for him. Making everything about him. And he couldn't show up for her this one time? When *she* needs him to study? To help *her*?

Oh, wow. Tay feels so foolish. And yeah, angry. Maybe Reece wasn't interested in Tay as a girlfriend, only what she could do for him: boost his ego. Which she's been doing over and over again. While she loves to cheer for others, it hurts when people can't give her a boost when she needs it.

And Reece has done the opposite: He's absolutely crushed her.

Tay rushes out of the Coffee Cave to find it pouring outside. She can't bike home in this weather. How did everything get so much worse in just a matter of minutes? It's the last thing she needs this week. She already has so much going on. Exam. Game. Dance.

Feeling lost, Tay calls the one person who's always been there for her. Who has never, ever let her down.

One who will be furious that his daughter has been abandoned. And was maybe right all along about Reece.

"Daddy?" she says through sobs when he picks up the phone.

"Baby girl, what's wrong?"

"He's not here. He's not coming, he's—"

"Say no more. I'll be right there."

Tay hides under an awning from the pouring rain, but it doesn't matter as her face is drenched with tears.

Here she thought she meant something to Reece. But you don't do this to someone you care about. A girlfriend. Even a friend.

So what is Tay going to do now?

As always, she'll take a lesson from Taylor Swift. The test. The game. The dance.

She's so good, she'll do it all with a breaking heart.

Our Chat (The Taylors Version)

TAY🎉: ARE YOU READY FOR SOME HIGH SCHOOL FOOTBALL?

TEFFY📚: I'll be cheering FOR YOU!

TAY🎉: Don't forget CHARLIE is also playing

TEFFY📚: Who?

TS⚽: BURN Teffy, you ICON 😂

TS⚽: Sorry I can't make it, need to concentrate on MY big game

TAY🎉: CAN'T WAIT, TS! I'm going to be SO LOUD you're going to wish I stayed home

TS⚽: Challenge accepted

TAYLOR🐝: Team Taylor UNITE!

TAY🎉: One . . .

TAYLOR🐝: Two . . .

TEFFY📚: Three . . .

TS⚽: LET'S GO TAYLORS!

NINETEEN

Now That We Don't Talk

"There you are!"

Teffy smiles at Taylor, who is waving her down from the crowded bleachers at the Homecoming game Friday night. If only one thing is going right for Teffy, she's glad it's the Taylors. Because having Taylor mad at you is no joke. She knows how to hold a grudge.

Not that Teffy isn't still worried about Hunter and what he could possibly do to Taylor's heart. But she doesn't want to rock the boat. So she's going to keep her mouth shut and hope for the best.

"I got us popcorn and I thought ahead and brought some pumpkin spice to put on it. I call it popcorn a la Teffy." Taylor holds out a bucket and Teffy happily dives in.

Because when Taylor's back to loving you, it's the best.

"It's not fall without a cozy cardigan and me eating everything and anything pumpkin spiced." Teffy wraps her blue-and-yellow Harrison Eagles scarf around her neck. "Aren't you cold?"

Taylor's wearing a short denim skirt with a red puffer jacket, and her legs are covered in goose bumps.

"Yeah, I should've worn tights, but I'm going to a party with Hunter after and those parties are always crowded and hot."

"Sounds like my worst nightmare. The party," Teffy clarifies quickly.

"Well, Hunter bought a gold tie to match my dress for tomorrow night, so I'll put up with his friends." Taylor looks around. "Where are your parents? I figured they'd be here to cheer on Charlie."

"Don't even get me started." Teffy shakes her head. Once again, the store comes first.

"And don't even get *me* started on *that*." Taylor moves her chin to the side, where Hannah is passing out VOTE FOR HANNAH buttons. She's wearing that MISS PRESIDENT sash again. Teffy has a feeling she'll be wearing it all year. "She doesn't even have anybody running against her, but heaven forbid she doesn't make everything about her."

Teffy glances at Taylor, and she knows she shouldn't press her since they're finally back on good terms, but she can't help it. "You would've won, you know."

Taylor gives Teffy a look that makes it clear she does know. "Yeah, well, it's too late. Today was the deadline to register."

"Hannah is going to be so insufferable now." Teffy actually shakes, not from the cold, but from the terror that will be Hannah Reed with power.

Taylor sighs. "What was she before if not insufferable?"

They laugh as the stand erupts in applause as the cheerleaders take to the field. Teffy and Taylor stand up to cheer for Tay, who is beaming as she runs out. Teffy wishes she could be as comfortable in front of hundreds of people, but the only time Teffy really feels like herself is when she's with the Taylors . . . and Liam.

But she won't allow herself to go down that road. It's a pavement lined with the broken pieces of her heart.

"Go, Charlie!" Teffy cheers, trying to be a good sister, as the football team takes the field.

"Oh, there's Liam!"

Teffy's stomach drops. Since her blowup with Liam last week, Teffy's been able to avoid him at school. She's stayed in her room with her drapes closed. It's been tempting to sneak a peak at Liam, but she has to protect herself.

Liam Yoon will never be hers.

"Look at Tay," Taylor says with awe as Tay rushes to the center of the field. She does a double back flip. And because that's not enough, she then does a split in midair.

Tay belongs where everybody can see her. And Teffy can't wait to share all the new songs she's been working on with her. Teffy likes having a partner, a muse, someone to perform the songs in her head.

"She's practically glowing," Teffy remarks as Tay beams.

This is her night as well.

Tay has been looking forward to the Homecoming game since she made the squad that first week of school. It's the biggest crowd of the year. It's supposed to be her moment to shine. Sure, Tay's all smiles and splits on the outside, but inside, she aches.

"Make sure your jumps are high and those smiles wide!" Cat claps to the squad. "We need all your energy for the team. One hundred percent!" Cat then does a kick. The rest of the cheerleaders fall in line, Tay included.

"Let's go, Eagles!" Tay shouts.

But why did Reece have to be such a jerk? screams inside her head.

Tay expected him to apologize to her today in class, but he refused to even acknowledge her, right before her biology test—which she doesn't even want to think about how she did. It's as if she was nothing to him.

She hasn't told the Taylors what happened because saying it out loud would make it real. She's already paid enough of a price for falling for Reece.

"Come on!" Tay says to the crowd, waving her pom-poms in the air. She throws in a high kick for good measure.

All Tay wanted to do was sing with Reece. To be part of his world. To feel his lips on hers again.

And he outright rejected her.

Tay has no idea how she'll handle the dance tomorrow night when she has to stand there and watch him perform the songs she helped pick out.

At least she doesn't have to pretend to like his moody songs anymore. And she can go back to wearing her bright colors.

The buzzer sounds across the field, signaling the game is about to start.

"Let's go, Liam!" Cat calls out as the starters take their positions.

Becca leans into Cat. "Things okay between you two?"

"Not now!" Cat snaps before putting on a big smile.

Hmm, perhaps Tay isn't the only one having to fake it.

"Louder, ladies!" Cat says to the squad.

Tay cheers, and her gaze automatically goes into the stands where Teffy and Taylor are. They catch her eye and start cheering for her.

It's just the boost Tay needs.

The game kicks off and the football goes sailing in the air. Liam catches it and starts sprinting toward the end zone.

Cat's screams are deafening, but the whole crowd is getting louder as Liam makes his way to score within the first few seconds. Liam is starting to break away from the others, but there's one opposing player catching up to him.

Liam is only a few yards away from a touchdown when he's tackled from the side and goes down hard.

A groan of disappointment comes from the stands, but the cheerleaders clap in encouragement.

But even those cheers start dying down as it's clear that something is wrong.

Liam isn't getting back up.

Teffy can hardly breathe. She's not the only one. The crowd has gone silent as she watches in horror as Liam remains on the ground. The coach, a few players, and Cat have all rushed to his side.

Teffy feels Taylor's hand in hers and she gives it a squeeze. She's frozen as Liam remains on the ground.

Please be okay, please be okay, Teffy repeats in her head. Sure, she can shut him out of her life to protect herself, but she'd do anything to keep him safe.

There's a burning in the back of her eyes and she wills Liam to move, to do something.

Then there's a wave of relief as Liam finally sits up. Teffy lets out a breath, but her lungs feel constricted. Taylor rubs her back as Teffy desperately tries to steady her breathing. Her eyes sting for a moment. The panic of something happening to Liam was too much. Even for a short moment.

Applause starts rippling through the crowd as Liam is helped off the field.

"You okay?" Taylor asks.

"Um, I . . ." Her focus is on Liam. She can't see his face because of his helmet, but his sunken posture and limp are too much.

"Teffy, if you want to go check on Liam, I understand."

"I . . . I can't." Teffy looks down at her hands and starts picking at her fingernails.

"Why can't you?" Taylor tilts her head. "He's one of your closest friends. Sure, he's not named Taylor, but he's cool."

"Well, we . . . sort of . . . got into a fight."

"What?" Taylor's mouth drops open. "But you're, like . . . perfect for each other. You're—" Taylor sits up straight and looks out to the field. Cat is by Liam's side as he leaves the field with his parents and Jae. "Oh my goodness. Teffy, you should be with Liam."

"He's got his family and Cat." He doesn't need her. At least the way she wants to be needed.

"No, Teffy, you should *be* with Liam. How am I just seeing this now?" Taylor hits her head with the palm of her hand. "It's like, duh, childhood sweethearts."

"Yeah, unfortunately, he doesn't see me that way."

"Well, boys are idiots," Taylor says with a loud laugh. Teffy really missed hanging with her. "You should go make sure he's okay. Listen, I'm speaking from experience—very recent personal experience, if you recall—heated words can be exchanged, but it's only because you care."

"Oh, it's just, um . . ." Teffy's not sure what to do.

She does care about Liam. Too much.

If anything ever happened to him . . .

Teffy has never felt such a weight on her heart.

Taylor puts her hands on Teffy's shoulders. "You know you're incredible, right? I know we tell you all the time how talented and special you are. How thoughtful. How you put others first. But I don't think you really believe it. You deserve to have whatever you want. And be with whoever you want. If you want to be with Liam, you need to fight for him. Now, go get your boy!"

Before Teffy can convince herself why it's a bad idea, she runs out of the stadium. She's a bundle of nerves on the way home, where she arrives to an empty house. It seems like hours and hours as she impatiently waits for Liam to get home. Finally, Mr. Yoon's car pulls into their driveway and Liam gets out using crutches. Cat is by his side.

Teffy runs out of her house. "Are you okay, Liam?"

"Tefs! Hey!" Liam's face lights up when he sees her. "I'm so glad to see you. Yeah, it's just a sprain. Listen, can we talk?"

Mr. and Mrs. Yoon get out of the car and pause when they see Teffy. But Jae comes running over and gives her a hug.

"Hey, Jae." Teffy holds on to Jae tightly.

"Where have you been, Teffy?" Jae looks up at Teffy with her big brown eyes.

"Oh, um." She sees Mr. and Mrs. Yoon studying her cautiously. Maybe they haven't told Jae what's going on since she's only twelve. Even though she's only a couple years younger, Teffy has always been protective of Jae, like a little sister. "Hi, Mr. and Mrs. Yoon."

Teffy hates that things are so stilted now. It's the Yoons! Teffy lost her first tooth over at their house on a caramel apple one year during Halloween. When they'd host barbecues, Mr. Yoon would put extra cheese on Teffy's burgers because he knows how much she likes cheese. Mrs. Yoon would clear out their living room so Teffy and Jae would have space to dance along to the Eras Tour movie.

Mrs. Yoon gives her a warm smile, one that Teffy misses. "Hey, Teffy, I want you to know that you're still welcome over at our house. We miss you. And I'm sorry things have been so difficult between us. But to clarify, it's between your parents and us, not you."

"Thanks." It means the world for Mrs. Yoon to say it aloud, if only Teffy's parents could be the same way.

"Come on, Jae." Mrs. Yoon gestures for Jae to go inside the house.

Teffy gives her another squeeze before she leaves. There's a silent pause as Cat stands next to Liam, her arms wrapped around herself, shivering in her cheerleader uniform.

Liam's gaze has remained on Teffy. "I'll be right inside, Cat. I need a minute with Tefs."

Cat looks between Liam and Teffy, her eyes narrow, and then she flips her hair. "Of course, of course! Well, I guess, I'll . . . go in." She sprints up to the door. "Bye, Tefs!"

Teffy has had over an hour to think about what to say to Liam, but standing with him in front of her, she's at a loss. While Taylor told her to fight for Liam, Teffy thinks what she really needs to do is tell him the truth. And deal with the consequences.

Liam hobbles closer to Teffy. "Tefs, I don't understand what's going on. What did I do? Please talk to me. We've always been able to talk to each other."

Teffy needs to stop with these fantasies. The ones where Liam will finally see her differently, but she at least needs to tell him how she feels. She needs to stop hiding. "You mean so much to me, Liam."

"Same here. Nobody puts up with me like you do." He gives her a bashful smile.

"But I don't think we mean the same thing to each other." Teffy's throat tightens as if she's too scared to have the words tumble out.

"What do you mean?" Liam looks genuinely confused. "Because I gotta be honest, Tefs. This—" He gestures to his ankle. "Didn't hurt nearly as much as you not talking to me."

Teffy realizes that the response to this question may pain her the most. "Liam, who am I to you?"

Liam looks confused. "What? You're Tefs! You're . . . the best."

"No, I'm not." She hates to admit it, but he's got Cat waiting for him inside his house.

"Of course you—"

"Stop." Teffy can feel the tears burning behind her eyes. "The thing is, Liam, I know how you see me. I'm good old reliable Teffy. The little sister. The one you'll never see as anything but a kid. But I don't see you like that . . . I like you, Liam. I can't pretend away my feelings anymore. And I know you've got your perfect girlfriend and your popular jock friends, while I'm just Teffy. The book nerd. The quiet one. The one you hang out with when *she's* not around."

"Wait." Liam blinks quickly like he's trying to compute everything Teffy has told him. "I—I—I don't—"

"I know you don't feel the same way, but can't you see, it's so hard for me to spend time with you, to feel the things I do when I know it won't be returned. I had to step away from you so I could take a sliver of my dignity back. And I—"

The front door opens and Cat stands in the frame. "Liam, it's cold and you need to elevate your leg. Doctor's orders."

"Yeah, just give me a minute," Liam replies abruptly.

Teffy waits for Cat to close the door before she continues. "Liam, I wish I could snap my fingers and change how I feel so we can go back to being just friends, but that's not how feelings work. I'm just glad you're okay and that you're happy."

"But, Tefs, I . . ." Liam seems out of breath. "I . . ."

"It's okay, Liam." Teffy couldn't bear to hear Liam say the words that he doesn't feel the same way. But that's how things are with Liam: She knows him so well, he doesn't need to say another word. "Look, I gotta go. Bye."

Teffy turns and rushes into her house, into her bedroom, and collapses on her bed.

Our Chat (The Taylors Version)

TS⚽: Just heard about Liam, he OK?

TEFFY📚: Just a sprain.

TS⚽: Phew

TAYLOR🐝: Are YOU okay, Teffy?

TEFFY📚: Yep.

TAY🎉: And are we all ready for THE MOST IMPORTANT GAME TOMORROW?

TAYLOR🐝: THE BIGGEST

TEFFY📚: THE BEST!

TS⚽: Dear Taylors, thank you for acknowledging my team's greatness

TAY🎉: And we can't wait to hear about your senior party tonight, Taylor

TS⚽: She's in the big leagues

TWENTY

Dear Reader

Taylor hugs her phone, grateful for her friends, even though she wishes Teffy had dished on whatever happened with Liam. She's going to ask Teffy so many questions tomorrow during TS's game. Taylor wants to know every single detail.

Unfortunately, it's not just Teffy who has gone silent.

Game's over. Where are you? Taylor messages Hunter, scrolling through the twenty-six—*twenty-six!*—messages she sent him during the game. He was supposed to pick her up twenty minutes ago.

Taylor goes out into the parking lot, watching other people leave with friends. While she's just standing there, hoping Hunter will finally materialize, as the parking lot empties.

Honestly, his phone probably ran out of battery. He's always forgetting to charge it.

"Hey, Taylor!" Taylor turns around to see Amina, the girl who gave her a ride home from the lake. "You good? Need another ride?"

"Oh, hey, um . . ." What if Taylor leaves and then Hunter shows up? He'll be annoyed that he came all the way to get her if she's not here. But *he's* not here. Or answering her texts.

"You going to Stephen's? Because that's where we're headed,"

Amina says while her friends—all seniors—get in her car.

"Yeah." Taylor looks down the road, wondering if Hunter is stuck in traffic, but the road is fairly empty.

"Because that's where Hunter is," Amina fills in for her.

"Oh. He's supposed to get me," Taylor says in such a small voice, she hardly recognizes it as her own. When did she get small? When did she become so unsure of herself? When did she start questioning everything?

Although, the questions keep coming: Why didn't Hunter tell Taylor he was already at the party? Does that mean he's not coming? She would know if he would get back to her. How hard is it to send one text?

Taylor grimaces. The thing is, Taylor loves being in a relationship with Hunter. What's not to love: He's gorgeous, he's kind, he listens to her . . . But she also doesn't really know what she's doing. Having a boyfriend is new to her. Taylor has no idea what she's supposed to do now. Go with Amina and her friends? Wait for Hunter?

The window rolls down and a guy Taylor recognizes from another party pops his head out. "From the pics I've seen from the party, Hunter's not going anywhere."

The three people in the back seat all laugh, making Taylor want to disappear. Now she doesn't even want to go to this stupid party, but if she doesn't show, Hunter will probably get mad.

Ugh. This uncertainty.

All Taylor knows is that everything is better when she's with

Hunter. Once she gets to the party and he puts his arm around her, all this discomfort will be worth it. All this questioning will be forgotten.

"Yeah, a ride will be great." Taylor forces a confident smile before getting in the front seat.

She's introduced to the three in the back and tries to remember their names, but she's too focused on pretending that everything's fine. *It* will *be fine once you find Hunter*, she reminds herself.

"How long have you been with Hunter?" one of the girls in the back asks.

"Oh, pretty much from the start of school," Taylor replies.

It's been over a month. One amazing month. Sure, there were a couple little blips, but Taylor has learned so much from Hunter. She knows she needs to let him have his space, especially when he's with his friends. She doesn't insert herself into conversations. She speaks when spoken to.

Be a little less than yourself, a voice echoes in her head.

No, she's learning to be a couple. A relationship. A *real* relationship.

It can't always be about Taylor. She's not Hannah.

"And you're a freshman?" a guy asks as he purses his lips.

"Yes."

There's a giggle between them when the same guy says in an exaggerated Southern accent, "That's the thing about these freshman girls, man. Hunter gets older, but they stay the same age."

They all break out in laughter while Taylor shrinks in her seat. She's so sick of the jokes about their age difference.

Taylor keeps her eyes glued to the road and her mouth shut until they reach the party. It takes everything in Taylor to not rush into the house and right into Hunter's arms. She follows Amina inside, where music is blasting and people are crowded around a table, with more people dancing in the middle of the living room.

Hunter is nowhere to be found.

As Taylor makes her way around the house, searching for Hunter, she pretends to ignore the looks, the murmurs. One girl not even subtly points to Taylor, and then whispers in her friend's ear.

Amina comes from behind her. "That's Jodie, Hunter dated her last year when she was a freshman," she explains. Amina gestures at another girl across the room. "Then he dated Sadie, also as a freshman. And there's Abby—"

The girl who went up to Taylor that very first day and warned her about Hunter. "Let me guess, Abby also dated Hunter when she was a freshman."

"Hunter has a type." Amina gives Taylor that look she's used to getting from his friends: pity.

But here's the thing: If Hunter was this awful person, why would they be friends with him?

Exactly.

Abby comes up to Taylor. "So . . . I see you didn't listen."

"Yeah, well, I'm glad I didn't," Taylor fires back at her. "I would never take advice from an ex, anyways. And you should know Hunter and I are *very* happy."

She cocks one eyebrow. "Why don't you go upstairs? That's where I last saw Hunter heading."

"I will." Taylor marches up the flight of stairs. She can't wait to see Hunter. She doesn't mind the glances and whispers when she's in his arms.

The small hallway upstairs is oddly quiet. As she takes hesitant steps, she feels like she's walking into some kind of trap. She presses her ear against one of the closed doors and hears the laughter of a girl. Taylor is about to move to the next door when Hunter's voice rings out.

Finally! Taylor smiles as she opens the door, excited to see Hunter.

It takes Taylor a minute to process what she sees happening in the room. Hunter is there. But he's kissing someone else. Not just anybody, it's Kim Cohen from her freshman English class. Hunter and Kim are too wrapped up in each other to notice Taylor.

There's a part of her that wants to run and pretend she didn't see this. That this isn't happening.

Because it *can't* be happening.

"Hunter?" Taylor calls out. Hoping that her mind is playing tricks on her. Because this can't be Hunter. Her Hunter who *loves* her.

Hunter blinks at Taylor for a moment, like he almost doesn't recognize her. She's waiting for him to start explaining. To apologize and grovel. To do something to make up for this.

Instead, Hunter does the last thing Taylor expected. He laughs. Is this some sort of joke? A prank? Because Taylor doesn't find any of this funny.

No, in fact, it's the opposite of funny. She's breaking apart inside.

"Why are you laughing?" Taylor asks, surprised at how calm her voice is. She feels like she's underwater. Everything is muted. Her body feels heavy.

"Are you going to cause another scene?" Hunter puts his arm around a stunned Kim. "Learn from Taylor on what *not* to do, babe."

Babe. What he calls Taylor. She thought she was his. No, wait, he *told her* she was his. Her *told her* he *loved* her. He didn't want to share her with anybody—her friends, even running for class president—but he can have another girl.

"I don't understand." Taylor finds herself shaking. "I did everything you asked." Because she loved him. Because she thought he loved her.

"Well, apparently it wasn't enough." He gets up from the bed and goes over to a mirror to tuck in his shirt, while Kim sits there uncomfortably. "Listen, it was fun and all, but I'm just not really feeling it anymore, you know?"

"What does . . ." Then it happens. Taylor starts to cry. Not just a little tear, but an ugly sob of pure agony erupts from within her.

She was warned. By Abby that first day. By Teffy. One of her best friends! And Taylor was so awful to Teffy. Taylor ignored everybody else because she wanted to believe in Hunter.

"Oh, please." Hunter actually rolls his eyes at her tears. "You're so predictable."

"Well, well, I—I—I—" Taylor stutters between sobs. She gave up so much for him and this is what she gets?

"I—I—I—" Hunter repeats with a laugh. "Taylor, it's over. I'm into someone else." He sits back down and pulls Kim into his lap. She gazes at him with that lovesick look that Taylor used to have.

Taylor opens her mouth to warn her but knows it won't work since it didn't work on her.

Taylor didn't listen.

She also knows Hunter won't listen to her. Because he doesn't care about her. He probably never did. She was just this young thing he could control. Who did what he said.

And she fell for it.

Sadness morphs into anger as Taylor turns around and storms out of the house. Taylor's mind starts swirling, not solely with how she's going to get home, but how she'll get back at Hunter. She needs to let the entire world—or at least the students of Harrison High—know what kind of jerk Hunter Brown is.

Hunter Brown has underestimated the fury of a Taylor Swift fan scorned . . .

Our Chat (The Taylors Version)

TAYLOR🐝: thanks for the emergency video call 🖤🖤🖤

TS⚽: I'm gonna picture that jerk's face when I kick the ball tomorrow

TAY🎉: KICK IT EXTRA HARD FOR ME

TEFFY📚: And me.

TS⚽: We got you Taylor

TAYLOR🐝: Thanks . . . I'm moving on

TAYLOR🐝: And we have YOUR back tomorrow, TS

TEFFY📚: And I've got the best dates for the dance tomorrow.

TAY🎉: EAT YOUR HEART OUT, HARRISON HIGH!

TAYLOR🐝: Especially one cheating jerk

TEFFY📚: He messed with the wrong Taylors.

TS⚽: Look at Teffy! Getting into revenge mode is just the extra motivation I need

TEFFY📚: . . . READY FOR IT?

TS⚽: BRING IT

TWENTY-ONE
Hits Different

Most people get nervous before a big game.

If it wasn't already obvious, TS is not like most people.

She knocks on Coach Callahan's door before the game. "You wanted to see me, Coach?"

While TS hasn't been practicing with the starting squad since her meltdown, she's sure Coach is going to have her start today. It's the big game, they need her. She knows how to play big.

"Have a seat, Shaw." Coach motions toward the chair in her tiny office.

"I'd prefer to stand. Keep my body warm." TS shakes her legs out. She even ran to the field from home.

Coach leans back in her chair. "You've really gotten back into your head the last few days. It can be tough for an athlete to do, but you did it."

"I hope you can trust me when I say it was a fluke. I'm not one for drama." (Even though, hi, it's TS, she's the drama, that's her.) "I am more than ready for today."

"I know you are." She waits a beat. "But I'm not starting you."

"What?" TS can't believe it. She wants to protest, to fight, but she doesn't want to dig her hole even deeper.

"You've got the drive and determination, but there are ten other players on that field. You've been too focused on yourself. I know how much soccer means to you, but when you have something else outside of it, it might not make you a better player, but it'll make you a better *teammate*."

"But . . ." TS loves being part of a team. To have a group of people with a common goal, who have one another's back. Like the Taylors. But TS knows Coach Callahan is right. She's been working on *her* speed, *her* dribbling, *her* kicks, and not the team's.

She's been blocking them out, especially one teammate.

"You know what I like about Gemma," Coach continues as if she could read TS's mind. "She's an amazing technical player, but she also goes out there and enjoys herself. She's not concerned about her stats, she's there for the team. You two work really well together, or at least you used to. Not sure what's going on there, but you need to fix it."

"Of course."

Coach pauses for a moment, then a smile spreads on her face. "And to be clear, Shaw, I'm not just talking about soccer."

"Oh." Perhaps TS isn't as good at concealing her feelings as she thought. "Okay, thanks, Coach." TS goes to leave, but Coach calls after her.

"One more thing, Shaw, keep those legs warm. It's going to be a tough game."

♥♥♥♥

TS is going to approach pregame differently. Gone are her headphones. Instead of blocking everybody out, she checks in on her teammates.

"You've got this, Charlotte!" TS pats the back of the junior who will be starting in her place. "You've gotten so fast, I'm having trouble keeping up."

Charlotte gives her a grateful smile as she starts warming up.

TS glances at Gemma, but she's been busy talking to Shanti.

"Hey, Shaw." Phoebe, a senior who made all-state last year, comes over. "How do you do that one move to get around a defender?"

"Ah, the Ronaldo Chop! Let me show you." TS takes the ball and does the move—where she jumps forward into the ball, then kicks it behind her opposite leg—a few times. With each pass, more teammates have gathered around to watch, except Gemma, who remains seated by herself.

While her teammates are busy practicing, TS realizes she is going to have to swallow her pride and rip the bandage off.

"Got a second?" TS says to Gemma.

Gemma looks up and TS feels her breath catch as she looks into Gemma's big eyes. "Oh, you're talking to me again?"

"Yeah, I'm really sorry, Gemma. I got into my head, *you* got into my head. And—"

"Yes, you made it pretty clear how *I* am the one to blame." Gemma frowns, and there's a look TS has never seen on her face: disappointment. Hurt. TS knows she did that.

"No, I mean—" TS fumbles over her words.

"Look, Shaw, we've got a big game, yeah? So maybe we should just—"

"I really like you!" TS says so loudly the rest of the team gets quiet, save a couple teammates making "wooo" sounds. TS doesn't need to look in a mirror to know her face matches her hair. She keeps her voice low, even though everybody is staring at them. "I never had anything in my life outside of the Taylors and sports. Then you came along, and it's not like there's a playbook on what to do when the most amazing girl you've ever met comes into your life. So I fumbled. Big-time. I got too distracted by you, because how could I not? You're amazing, but then I blamed you when I messed up, which wasn't fair. So maybe you can help me find some middle ground, because I want to be there for you as a teammate and maybe, if I didn't totally wreck whatever it is between us, something more."

TS takes a deep breath, her heart practically thumping out of her chest.

"Time to hit the field!" Coach calls out. The other players head out of the locker room, leaving TS and Gemma alone.

"You sure know how to add even more tension before the biggest game of the season." Gemma stands and holds out her hand to TS. "Just follow my lead, yeah?"

"Wait, does that mean—?"

"Match first, Shaw, *then* we can talk about us after. Balance, right? This is how we do it: We win and then we figure this out."

TS has never wished a game to finish before it ever started, but then again, she's never had such an after to look forward to.

"Let's bring it in," Coach says before the start of the game. "We're going to—" She lifts her head up. "What on earth is that noise?"

The crowds at the girls' matches are usually pretty quiet, but as the team looks up at the stands, TS starts laughing. There are the three other Taylors dressed in blue and gold, waving pom-poms. They're standing in the front row doing a cheer from their time on the cheerleading squad in middle school.

TS holds up heart hands to her friends, which just makes them cheer even louder.

"Let's try to match that energy, team!" Coach says as she puts her hand in the center. Each of her teammates follows and TS puts hers on top of Gemma's. "'Eagles' on three. One . . . Two . . . Three!"

"EAGLES!" the team calls out, while TS mentally adds a *Let's go, TS!*

"Go get 'em, team!" TS shouts as she claps her teammates on when they take the field.

While TS sits and watches.

For nearly sixty minutes, TS does everything to support her teammates, even when the Lincoln Lions score, even when Charlotte gets an unfair yellow card, even through Coach's rough speech during the half as they're down by one. She even joins her team in a celebration dance when Emma scores the tying goal with five minutes left.

Five minutes.

"Shaw!" Coach calls over to TS. "You ready?"

"More than!" TS jumps to work out her nerves and get her legs warm.

The whistle blows and TS takes to the field, replacing a tired Charlotte. TS can hear the Taylors screaming her name. It's quite possible they're even louder than they were back at Lucas Oil Stadium, which is saying a lot.

The Lions get possession of the ball, not giving the Eagles a chance to get it back. TS has been staying on the opposing players, but they're fast. If something doesn't happen soon, they'll tie, or worse, the Lions will find a way to score. They've kept up their hustle through the second half. TS understands why they won state last year, but TS also knows her team is better. Especially when they work together.

Out of the corner of her eye, she sees that familiar flash of pink as Gemma breaks away and gets control of the ball.

"Go! Go! Go!" Coach screams from the sides as the entire team goes running down the field to try to score with less than two minutes left.

The crowd is going wild—and without looking, TS can tell 90 percent of the noise is from the Taylors. But everything is muted as TS's focus shifts to the ball that's being passed between her teammates. She tries to get open, but the Lions are working hard on defense. TS fakes going left and then rushes right to get closer to the goal, but there's a surge of players.

Gemma kicks the ball and it's like slow motion as it sails toward the goal but bounces off the post, heading right to TS, who jumps up and uses her head to knock the ball back toward the goal and . . . it sinks into the back of the net.

GOAL!

Gemma runs up to TS and jumps into her arms. The rest of their teammates quickly follow. TS is crushed by her teammates congratulating her, but TS is sure to thank and cheer them on as well. They've been hustling for most of the game. She just happened to be in the right place at the right time. Seconds later the whistle blows, signaling the end of the game, and the field is rushed by Coach and her fellow teammates.

"You did it!" Gemma says as she squeezes TS even tighter.

"*We* did it." TS rubs her head where the ball hit. See? There are benefits to being hardheaded.

The Taylors are next in the flood of well-wishers.

"Look what they made you do!" Tay sings as she jumps up into splits. Teffy hugs TS, while Taylor is dancing around with her pompoms, chanting her name.

"You were amazing!" Teffy says with the biggest smile TS has seen from her in a while.

"Yay, sports!" Taylor does a little kick, but it's nowhere near as high as Tay's.

The four Taylors form a little group hug. "Pizza?" Tay asks.

"Like I'm ever going to say no to pizza." TS looks over to where

Gemma is talking to Coach. "I just have one more thing to do."

Teffy smiles, then gives her a little nudge. "Go get her, TS."

"What?" Tay starts, but then her eyes get wide. "Oh, YES! Go, TS!" She does another kick.

Taylor lets out a laugh. "Oh, TS, you old romantic, you."

TS rolls her eyes, but she's happy her best friends are so supportive.

"Well!" Tay gestures over at Gemma, and not even subtly. Not like Tay understands subtlety. "What are you waiting for?"

What *is* she waiting for? With a deep breath, TS heads over to Gemma, who is packing up her water bottle and shin guards.

"Hey," TS starts. "It's after the game."

"Yes, it is." Gemma raises a curious eyebrow.

Then TS says the words that have been stuck in her throat for days. "If you're willing to forgive me for being a horrific teammate this week, I would hope you'd do me the favor of coming with me to the Homecoming dance, not just as a friend, but as my date."

Then TS witnesses a far better sight than the ball going into the goal. Gemma's face bursts into a bright smile. "Why, Shaw, I thought you'd never ask."

Let the games begin.

Our Chat (The Taylors Version)

TAYLOR🐝: So full, I may not fit into my dress 🍕🍕🍕

TAY🎉: Should I tell my dad to NOT bake cookies?

TEFFY📚: There's always room for cookies.

TS⚽: I'm bettin' we eat them all, even though I'm full from WINNING

TAYLOR🐝: Just wait until we make our entrance

TAY🎉: GAH! WHAT IS TAKING YOU ALL SO LONG? GRAB YOUR STUFF AND GET OVER HERE NOW!

TWENTY-TWO

So High School

Dads can be *so* embarrassing.

"Are you *crying*?" Tay asks as she puts her head in her hands.

Her father wipes his face. "You all are just so beautiful and grown-up."

Tay looks at her friends, who are lined up for pre-dance photos. They have grown and been through so much since they first met in fifth grade. It's been four years, and she knows they'll have many more memories together.

Tay goes over to give him a hug. "You're such a softie."

He clears his throat. "No, I'm not. I'm tough."

"So tough," Tay mimics her dad with a smile.

"Your mother would be so proud," her dad whispers in her ear, and *that* nearly makes Tay burst into tears as well. She holds on tightly to her dad.

"Gah! Can someone help me with this?" TS breaks the mood as she fiddles with her headband.

"Come here, Shaw." Gemma tucks some of TS's hair under her black sparkly headband, which goes perfectly with the deep green vest she's paired with black satin shorts.

"Let's get a picture of just you two girls." Tay's dad sniffs as he snaps a picture of TS and Gemma, who is wearing a strapless mini dress that matches her pink hair.

"So cute!" Tay coos at the couple. Her own dress is very *Lover*-inspired: a light blue satin crop top with a baby pink tulle skirt. She wasn't the only one who took inspiration from Taylor Swift. Teffy is wearing a *folklore*-worthy dress in plum with a flowy skirt and puffy sleeves. Of course, Taylor couldn't resist her own moment in a gold flapper dress.

"One more with the whole crew," TS says as the group gets in for a few more shots. "We do polish up real nice."

"Too bad Reece couldn't be here," Taylor tells Tay.

"That boy is not welcome in this house," Tay's dad says with an actual growl.

So yeah, Tay still hasn't told the group about Reece ghosting her. She was going to and then Taylor had that whole nightmare with Hunter and then she didn't want to make TS's game about her drama.

Teffy looks between Tay's dad and a silent Tay. "What happened?"

"It's nothing," Tay says brightly, trying to not let anything ruin their evening.

"Do not play it off," her dad says between gritted teeth. "That boy stood up my baby girl and then, like the coward he is, didn't apologize."

"What?" Taylor sits down on the couch and taps the space next to her. "I can't believe you didn't tell us. Spill."

Tay remains standing, wanting to make it seem like it isn't a big deal, even though it is.

"Honestly, I didn't want . . ." to admit how hurt she was. "I just needed to concentrate on my test and the game and I knew you all had a lot going on and I . . ." didn't want to face the truth: She and Reece were over. They hadn't even had a chance to really begin. "I think he wanted me for my big mouth more than he wanted . . . me."

"Oh, Tay." TS wraps her arms around her. "We're here for each other no matter what, remember."

"Yeah." Teffy puts her arms around Tay's waist, her chin on her shoulder. "And we can stand in the back or sit outside during his set tonight."

"You guys are the best." Tay gives them both a squeeze.

Taylor stands up to wiggle her hips so her dress fans out. "Oh, we know. The absolute best." She then pulls Teffy into a hug. "And if boys, and I do mean *boys*, don't see what's right in front of them, they are not worth our time."

Tay's phone starts to ping with notifications from the cheerleader group chat. She goes to check her messages and she can't help but smile. "Well, well, well . . . It looks like Liam and Cat are no longer together."

The other Taylors look at a stunned Teffy.

"Oh, um . . ." Teffy blinks at the news.

"I totally take what I said back!" Taylor laughs. "Well, at least about Liam."

TS lets out a laugh. "Oh, this is going to be an epic night."

♥♥♥♥

Taylor knows how to walk into a room and command attention. And tonight, she feels wonderful. Confident. More like herself. Before that master manipulator came into her life.

Taylor needs that confidence because as soon as the Taylors enter the gymnasium, she notices a lot of the upperclassmen whispering and pointing at her.

"Let them stare," TS says. "You're gorgeous and better than him and the rest of them."

Yes, Taylor was hurt and devastated by Hunter's behavior and treatment of her, but she dusted herself off quickly. She doesn't have the writing talent like Taylor Swift—and Teffy—to get over a bad breakup, but she knows herself. Now that Hunter isn't in her way, Taylor can see how much more she's going to do. No putting her friends second. No more not prioritizing what Taylor wants. What Taylor *deserves*. And that is everything.

When the Taylors walk over to a balloon arch to get some pictures, Taylor notices Hunter is off to the side. Wearing the gold tie he bought for her. His arms around Kim. He catches Taylor out of the corner of his eye and plants a kiss on Kim's cheek.

Whatever. Taylor poses for the pictures, ignoring Hunter's gaze. As soon as they finish, Hunter goes straight for Taylor. He looks her up and down and her skin crawls.

That crooked smile that Taylor used to love spreads on his face. Now she knows it's not cute, it's conceited, just like him.

"I can't believe you have the nerve to show up," he says with a shake of his head.

"And *I* can't believe you'd be seen in public with that face," TS spits back at him, while Gemma laughs in delight.

Tay takes a step forward. "Just know, you mess with one of us, you get all of us."

Hunter smiles like he's enjoying this and not finding the Taylors the least bit threatening.

Big mistake, Hunter.

Teffy takes a hesitant step forward. "Let me make this clear: I'm quiet, but I will do everything in my power to destroy you."

Whoa. Who saw that coming from our quiet Teffy?

This gets Hunter to take a cautious step back.

"And I'm excluding myself from your narrative," Taylor replies with a hair flip as her friends follow her to the dance floor.

The DJ is playing an upbeat song, so they get in the center and start dancing. Gemma and TS twirl each other around, while Taylor enjoys making her dress swish. But there's this growing anger inside her that Hunter got away with what he did to her. What he's done to countless other girls.

"Okay, everybody," comes the voice of the principal from the stage. "Before the night gets away from us, just a few housekeeping notes." The crowd groans, but as he continues, Taylor starts thinking about what she can do to not only get back at Hunter but to get part of herself back. "A reminder that we have the upcoming student body elections and . . ."

"Taylor?" Teffy calls after Taylor as she walks with purpose toward the stage and then up the stairs and finds herself in front of the principal, who looks at her, confused.

"This will just take a minute," Taylor says as she takes the microphone away from the stunned principal. "Hi all, my name is Taylor Perez and I made a huge mistake. I was going to run for freshman class president and I didn't because I was told it would be a waste of time by someone who ended up being a waste of a human being. But here's the thing, standing up for yourself and others and fighting for what's right is never a waste. I know it's too late for my name to be on the ballot, but I'm asking for you to write in your vote for me, Taylor Perez, because I believe that girls' sports should have as many resources and celebrations as the boys'." There's applause from the crowd and loud cheers from TS and Gemma. "I believe that arts and literature are as important as sports and we need more funding." The crowd is now applauding more. "And that includes fighting book bans. Every voice deserves to be heard, so I want to make sure we have appropriate LGBTQ-plus representation on our bookshelves and in our meetings." Taylor has to raise her voice over the cheering from the audience. "And why is it the Homecoming King and Queen? What about our nonbinary royalty?"

Even the principal nods along to that one.

"A vote for Taylor Perez is a vote for all. And one more thing: I want to make sure freshmen have mentors to help them make a seamless transition to high school. It's important that we have people looking out for us. For instance, I should've listened to the upperclassman the first day who told me to stay away from Hunter Brown. Or the other girls he's dated . . . when they were freshmen. I believe the term is *grooming*? In fact, raise your hand if Hunter dated or hit on you when you were a freshman and he was not."

There's a shocking number of hands coming up from the audience, and Taylor spies an incredibly uncomfortable Hunter in the back. He takes in the raised hands and walks out of the gym.

"Okay, that's enough," the principal says to Taylor as he takes back the microphone.

"It certainly is." She walks to the front of the stage and throws her hands in the air. "Taylor for president!"

As she makes her way back into the crowd, Hannah runs toward her, wearing a tiara and a ridiculously poofy pink dress her parents probably got in Paris. "You can't just announce that you're running and ask people—"

Taylor holds her hand up. "Oh, just put it on a cupcake."

The applause continues and it has never sounded sweeter.

Tay is cheering the loudest she's ever cheered, which is saying a lot. Taylor is such a legend.

There's a tap on her arm and she turns to find Reece standing next to her, looking as cute as ever wearing all black, but a black shirt and tie and . . . he's wearing THE ARCHERS bracelet she made him.

"Do you have a second?" he asks.

TS comes over, her arms folded. "You okay, Tay? Because I can shut these dudes down alllll night."

Reece takes a step away, but then he faces TS. "I get it. I messed up, truly. If you want to hear me grovel, then it's fine, as long as I can talk to Tay."

TS's eyebrows go up in surprise, probably because it's the most she's ever heard Reece speak.

"Tay?" Reece pleads.

Tay nods as Reece gently guides her by the elbow to the corner of the gym.

"Yeah, I'm so sorry . . . I just . . ." He stops and looks down at the floor.

Tay clamps her mouth shut. She is not going to make this easy for him after what he's done to her. How rude and dismissive he was to her dad and friends. Tay is done filling in the silences for him.

But Reece isn't saying anything, just shifting on his feet.

"Ugh!" Tay lets out a groan. "This is not one of those times I'm going to talk for you, Reece. And for the record, it can be really tiring always putting in the work when it comes to hanging out. I ask you things, I want to know you, I want to spend time with you, and you run hot or cold. What do you want from me?"

"I'm so sorry. I'm not as good with speaking as you. I get nervous . . ." His eyes dart back up at Tay, but this time he doesn't look away. "I really do like you. When we're together, I can relax, because I can just be myself. I didn't think you minded when I was quiet, but I'll send you the list of a million things I want to know about you. I'm better at writing my feelings than speaking them."

"Then, what was the other night?" The sting of being stood up is still fresh in her mind.

"You know I take my music seriously, and well, when I heard Teffy's song—and how much you enjoyed singing it—it made me jealous. She's good, like, whoa, genius good, and I sort of spiraled."

Tay studies his face. She knows how sensitive he can be, but what he did was cruel. "You stood me up over a song?"

"I know, I'm an idiot. I made a mistake. A huge one. I get that now. And I don't know what else to say to you except that I'm sorry and I hope you can find it in that big heart of yours to forgive me." And then in the gym, in front of everybody under the twinkling lights, Reece gets down on his knees. "Please, Tay, I'm literally begging you. Forgive me. Please."

Tay wants to jump into his arms, but she's not sure she can trust him. Reece feels so much, but so does Tay.

And he broke her fragile heart.

"I'm going to need some time," she says once she's caught her breath.

Reece gently takes her hands. "Of course. I totally get it if you can't forgive me, but if you do, I'll never stop making it up to you. I'll always be there for you, Tay."

But you weren't there the other night, she wants to remind him.

Corey comes over. "Dude, we're almost up. Come *on*."

Reece's entire focus is on Tay.

"You should go," she tells him, but mostly to figure out what she's going to do.

He gets up and brushes off his knees. "Okay, please watch. I've got a surprise for you."

Like there was any way Tay would miss this.

"I told you I knew how to have fun," TS tells Gemma before she reaches her hand out to her. "Come on, let's get the room talking about us."

TS leads Gemma out on the dance floor as a slow song plays. She wraps her arms around Gemma and plants a kiss on her lips. TS didn't think there could be a feeling better than winning a game, but that was before she met Gemma. Before she knew how incredible it feels to find that someone who complements you. Who gets you. Who is utterly gorgeous and as unbelievably talented as Gemma.

"I've been thinking," TS begins.

"That sounds like it could be dangerous." Gemma pulls TS in closer, and TS buries her head in Gemma's hair for a moment, breathing in.

"I've been thinking that I can make dancing part of my cardio training, you know, a way to bring in the fun. And then this"—TS twirls Gemma around—"could be part of my cooldown."

"Or, you know, you could just dance to dance." Gemma shakes her head.

"That, too." TS wants this feeling—this hopeful, light, sparkling feeling—to stay with her. She realizes she needs to lighten up and knows just how to do it and, more importantly, who she can do it with. "And you should be aware that I don't plan on letting go of you tonight." TS pulls Gemma in tighter.

Gemma raises her eyebrows. "Babe, don't threaten me with a good time."

♥♥♥♥

The lights go down as the Archers take the stage. Taylor wraps her arms around Tay. "You good?"

"Yeah. Although probably not as good as TS," Tay jokes even though she's so happy for her friends. "And you! Getting those votes. I see you working the room."

"Got to give the people what they want." Taylor does another shimmy of her dress.

"Hannah is going to throw a tantrum."

"Added bonus!" Taylor gives her a wink.

"Hey, Harrison High," Reece says into the microphone. "We're the Archers and we're going to start with a song for one special person in the audience." Reece holds his hands up to his eyes as he scans the crowd, then his gaze settles on Tay. "This one's for you, Tay." Reece starts strumming the opening of "Love Story."

The Taylors all start dancing in a circle with Tay in the middle as Reece sings. He changes the Romeos and Juliets around, and it's almost as if Taylor Swift wrote this song for them, especially the part about the dad not approving.

Tay keeps going back and forth in her head about what to do. Forgive or move on. Fight this growing feeling or give in.

Then toward the end, Reece changes the lyrics again and starts repeating, *"Tay, just say yes."*

Tay looks out at her friends, all of them smiling at her, even Teffy.

"So?" TS asks as the song ends.

Before Tay can reply, Reece starts strumming his guitar again. "We'd like to invite a far superior singer up here to sing the next song with us."

The second she recognizes the song, Tay says, "Oh my."

"What a marvelous tune," Taylor finishes as she bumps her hip.

"Are you seriously going to turn down a chance to perform?" TS teases her.

But Tay looks at Teffy, wanting to make sure she'd be okay with it. Teffy gestures down at her outfit. "Tay, we're even dressed to the nines, you *have* to."

Adrenaline floods Tay as she heads to the stage. The second Reece sees her approaching, he flashes the biggest smile she's ever seen.

She walks over to him and gives him a nod. "I'm just saying yes to this song . . . for now."

"I'll take it!" Reece throws his fist in the air as the band starts the song again.

Tay starts singing the way *she* likes to sing. If she's going to perform, she's going to be herself. She walks over to the front of the stage, where the Taylors and Gemma have gathered, all singing along like it's the Eras Tour all over again. Tay has always wanted to be a star, but in this moment she truly feels like she's made of starlight.

Taylor has never felt better—about her future, about her friends—as she twirls around. She knows she has a lot of work ahead to get that presidency and to make some positive changes. She's going to be a force to be reckoned with when she becomes president. She'll be a fearless leader. She'll be the *girl*.

TS is already planning on all the new rituals and moments she'll be adding to her freshman year. She knows she needs to find balance between the fun and the focus. Luckily, she's got exactly what she needs wrapped up tightly in her arms: her London Girl.

Teffy is singing along when there's a tap on her shoulder. She turns around and is almost knocked over by the sight of Liam, looking as handsome as ever in a gray suit and purple tie, which nearly matches her own dress.

"Hey! Are you okay?" She gestures at his crutches.

"Yeah, you got a second?" Liam leans on his crutches enough to free his hands so he can take Teffy's into his. "You cut me off before, and I would like the opportunity to tell you exactly how I feel about you, Tefs."

How he feels . . .

Does that mean?

Teffy looks down at their entwined fingers and gives his hands a squeeze, just making sure this is really happening. Because this—Liam in his suit, holding her hands—is something she's dreamed about for so long. Could this be her reality?

Teffy can get carried away with her fantasies of being with Liam. She wants so much to think she could mean as much to him as he does to her. There's a feeling of hope fluttering around her body and landing squarely in her heart.

"Of course," Teffy replies, hoping he can't hear the nervousness in her voice.

As Teffy walks with Liam toward the back of the gymnasium, she tries to steady her breath, knowing that things are about to change, for better or worse.

Worst case: It'll make for great inspiration for a song. Best case: Her dreams are finally coming true.

As Liam stops and turns to Teffy with a look of determination on his face, Teffy can't help but wonder if this is when her love story will begin.

ACKNOWLEDGMENTS

File this project under my wildest dreams! *You want me to create characters with one of my best friends and listen to Taylor Swift all day and night and call it "work"? Um, SIGN ME UP!*

First, to David Levithan, who said to me during dinner one night, "Hey, so we have this project that I think you'd be perfect for . . ." Thank you for knowing me all too well!

To Maya Marlette—my Jack Antonoff! Your enthusiasm and editorial notes make everything I do better. I know these tight deadlines were also rough on you! I was NOT on my own, kid.

Have to also shout out Jen Calonita again. For being so open to my suggestions and asks on the chapter songs. And for carrying the description load. Tay's house is way better for it. Hey, kids, working together on a book is fun!

Kate Testerman, my agent, who loved this idea as much as me, and also for dealing with my freak-outs over the deadlines. (Y'all, long story short, it was a lot.)

It's nice to have an incredible team over at Scholastic. Your enthusiasm for this project since day one has meant the world to me. Special thanks to Aleah Gornbein, Lizette Serrano, Maisha Johnson,

Stephanie Yang, Erin Slonaker, Jessica Rozler, Brooke Shearouse, Seale Ballenger, Mary Kate Garmire, Maddy Newquist, Joy Simpkins, Lara Kennedy, and Lori Lewis.

Liz Parkes, thank you for bringing the story of the Taylors to life through your amazing illustrations!

Dear Reader, I'm assuming if you've read this book, you're also a Swifie. I'm no Taylor Swift (who is?), but I did my best to be a Mastermind and put in some fun Easter Eggs throughout. Happy hunting!

Last, but certainly not least, I have to thank Taylor Swift. For giving me (and the world) the absolute joy that was the Eras Tour. For your music. For making me a better writer by studying your lyrics. For being an absolute inspiration. I can't wait to see where your next era takes you. I am . . . ready for it.

ABOUT THE AUTHOR

Elizabeth Eulberg is the internationally bestselling author of dozens of books for young readers, including *The Lonely Hearts Club*, *Better Off Friends*, and most recently, *Take a Chance on Me*. But let's be real, you want to know her Swiftie credentials. She was gifted Debut ON CD, so she's a real one. Elizabeth first saw Taylor Swift perform in New Jersey (where Elizabeth used to live) in 2015 during the 1989 World Tour. Then, on August 19, 2024, she saw the Eras Tour at Wembley Stadium in London (where she now lives). Her surprise songs were "Long Live" x "Change" on guitar (SHE KNOWS!!) and "The Archer" x "You're On Your Own, Kid" on piano. She has still not fully recovered.

CAN'T GET ENOUGH OF THE TAYLORS? FLASH BACK TO SEE HOW IT ALL BEGAN!

A MIDDLE GRADE NOVEL BY JEN CALONITA

Taylor (aka Teffy to her family) is terrified to start middle school, that is until she makes friends with three other girls named Taylor and things start looking up! But then a surprise betrayal changes everything. How can their new friendship survive?

RELIVE *LOVE STORIES* WITH THIS CHAPTER TITLE PLAYLIST OF TAYLOR SWIFT SONGS!

the 1

Fifteen

Treacherous

A Place in this World

You're On Your Own, Kid

You Belong With Me

So It Goes . . .

Paper Rings

Stay Stay Stay

How You Get The Girl

invisible string

mad woman

Mastermind

Jump Then Fall

Untouchable

hoax

Electric Touch

Glitch

Now That We Don't Talk

Dear Reader

Hits Different

So High School

DON'T MISS ANOTHER LOVE STORY FROM ELIZABETH EULBERG!

Evie is heartbroken and betrayed when a video of her confronting her cheating ex-boyfriend goes viral, but as she explores London for the summer she finds herself repeatedly running into a charming and beautiful British busker named Aiden. Could he be worth taking a chance on?